the runners

FIACHRA
SHERIDAN

NEW
ISLAND

THE RUNNERS
First published 2009
by New Island
2 Brookside
Dundrum Road
Dublin 14

www.newisland.ie

Copyright © Fiachra Sheridan, 2009

The author has asserted his moral rights.

ISBN 978-1-84840-038-2

Book design by Inka Hagen

Printed in Ireland by Colourbooks Ltd

New Island received financial assistance from
The Arts Council (An Chomhairle Ealaíon), Dublin, Ireland.

10 9 8 7 6 5 4 3 2 1

For Denise

'Keep love in your heart. A life without it is like a
sunless garden when the flowers are dead.'

Oscar Wilde

Acknowledgments

This book would not have been written were it not for
the decisions of a few people: Warren Buffet,
Ronan Ivory and Sean Spillane.

Deirdre O'Neill, whose support and guidance was vital
in producing the final manuscript.

Máire O'Higgins, the believer.

Deirdre Nolan, the visionary.

Edwin, and all at New Island.

Faith O' Grady, Alison Walsh, Claire Rourke,
Edwina Forkin and all who read early drafts
and offered advice.

Especially my mam and dad, for all
their love and expertise.

CHAPTER 1

Bobby's house was closer than any other to Croke Park, Ireland's biggest sports stadium. He would stare out his bedroom window at the Cusack Stand, dreaming of the day eighty thousand people would come to see him playing football for Dublin. His brother, Kevin, slept on the top bunk. Kevin was three years older than Bobby at fifteen. He was in secondary school. Bobby had the summer holidays to go before he started in big school. There would be girls in his class for the first time. Kevin and Bobby were completely different. Kevin played guitar and hung around with his friends in Clontarf, one of the poshest areas of Dublin. Bobby played sport and hung around all over Dublin's north inner city, one of the poorest parts of Dublin, with his best friend, Jay.

Bobby's mam, Laura, was from Clontarf. Bobby's dad, Matt, was from Ballybough. His father had been called Matt after Matt Busby, the great Manchester United manager. When they got married, money dictated that a house in Ballybough was all they could afford. Laura wasn't happy living beside the flats. Only a mile away in Clontarf were gorgeous houses by the beach. Most of the houses on Ballybough Road were boarded up. Bobby's dad said he could make money restoring them, but he never did. The boarded-up windows didn't keep Bobby and Jay out. They would have hours of fun in a derelict house. They would have tightrope walking competitions on the exposed beams of the upper floor. They would catch pigeons and release them and they would light fires in the old buildings that once housed families of ten and more in each room, with just one outdoor toilet between them. Bobby knew all about the history of the tenement buildings. Jay didn't care.

Bobby's dad was on the social welfare. He collected seventy-five pounds a week because he was an unemployed builder. He would get up every day and look for work, but there was none. Bobby wasn't sure if he looked at all. Bobby knew that seventy-five pounds a week was ten pounds seventy-one pence a day, with three pence left over. A pint of Guinness was just under a pound. Bobby's dad loved Guinness. 'The nicest drink in the world,' he would say. He always got asked the same question when he got home.

'How many pints did you have?'

'Two or three.'

How could it be two or three, thought Bobby. It had to be one or the other.

Jay lived in the flats, and Bobby considered the huge flats complex beside his house his real home. The flats were built so people could move out of the cramped tenement buildings that were now all boarded up. Jay lived on the top floor. His bedroom window looked out over the Royal Canal, the railway tracks and Ballybough Bridge. Bobby's mam said Jay had a cheeky smile. Jay's dad was in prison and his mother, Bernie, was a trader on Moore Street in the city centre. She was the youngest of all the fruit sellers. She was tall and thin and attractive. She had straight, blonde hair and never wore any make-up. Bobby fancied her, but had never told Jay. Any men that bought fruit or veg on Moore Street bought it from Bernie. Her good looks drew them in. She was friendly and flirty and they all thought she fancied them.

'Here they are, looking for money again. Have a banana instead, son.'

'I hate bananas, Ma. Can I have twenty pence?'

'They're full of goodness. Eat a banana and I'll give you twenty pence.'

Jay didn't really hate bananas. He just knew his ma would make him eat one in front of all the oul wans. They thought it was hilarious.

'He is so cute, that young fella of yours, Bernie.'

Bobby would have eaten a banana for twenty pence. That was four games of Mario Brothers.

They always ate bananas before training. Anto said they were full of carbohydrates. Anto was the most recognisable person in Ballybough. He had a big mop of blond hair. Bobby could see an aura around him. Jay didn't know what an aura was. Bobby thought most people were miserable. Anto was always happy. He would say hello to every person he met. Bobby and Jay thought it was weird that he would say hello to people he didn't know. Anto said 'it always pays to be nice'. Most twenty-nine-year-olds were on the social welfare. Anto didn't have time to sign on the dole. He was too busy running the boxing club.

The boxing club was a different world. It had a distinct smell of sweat and leather and the freezing cold gave you goosebumps, even in the middle of summer. The boys had to train hard before they were even allowed in the ring. If you could attain a good level of fitness, which would be assessed by Anto, then you could fight. Bobby and Jay would always fight each other because they were both about the same age and the same weight. The gloves they wore were club gloves. That meant that hundreds of boys had worn them. If you had to put them on after another boy, the inside would be saturated in sweat. If you put them up to your nose, the smell would kill you. Jay and Bobby would jog the two miles to the gym, which was just off Moore Street. Anto would put them through their paces, starting with skipping, followed by sit-ups, press-ups and stretching. He said they had to do it if they wanted to be champions. All the boys trained in pairs. When it came to the punch-bag, it was thirty seconds on, thirty seconds off. If Bobby said he was tired, Jay would slag him.

'I'm going to knock you out when we get in the ring, I feel really strong.'

Jay would dance around, shadow boxing. He would throw punches at Bobby, stopping the glove a few inches from his face every time. Bobby always concentrated before a fight, even if it was just training. Jay would always act the clown. Sometimes Bobby would pretend he was tired so he could fool Jay into overconfidence.

'There's no point in saving it for the ring, Jay. I'm going to knock you out.'

Neither of them had ever managed a knock-out. Anto would only let them box for one minute at a time and he never let them go flat out. They were well-matched, so they hurt each other without ever inflicting real pain.

'I want to remind everyone that we are leaving early next Saturday morning. We have two boxers left who have a chance to qualify for the All-Ireland finals,' Anto announced.

The six other young boxers all stared at Bobby and Jay. They looked up to them because they were by far the best young boxers in the club. Anto told them they were two of the best boxers in the country for their age. Bobby had known about the away trip for a while and hadn't given Anto an excuse as to why he couldn't go.

'My ma says we don't have the money.'

'Don't worry about the money, it's already taken care of.'

Maybe he just wouldn't show up for the bus.

'I'll be starting the engines at half six in the morning. If you're late we're leaving without you,' added Anto. 'I've arranged for all of you to get a bout. We're fighting at Mayfield Boxing Club. The Cork lads will be looking forward to boxing the heads off you Dublin boys, so be prepared.'

The real competition for Bobby and Jay came after they left the gym. They always raced home. There was always a winner in a running race. They would start off at a slow pace, but when they reached the Sunset House pub it was flat out all the way to the bridge over the canal, and the downhill finish that took them to the top of Sackville Avenue. There was never more than a few yards in it, as both of them had good sprint finishes. The two of them would walk the length of the avenue to get their breath back, the winner gloating about being the best, and the loser making up excuses for the defeat.

The flats were all three storeys high. Each landing had seven flats. Twenty-one flats in each building. Sixty-three flats on Sackville Avenue. The ground-floor flats were single storey. They were designed for old people. A round stairwell led you to the upper floors. Anto lived on the top floor of the middle block with his granny. Bobby and Jay never asked why he didn't live with his mam and dad, or ma and da, as Jay would say. Bobby would say ma and da too, but if his mother heard him she would correct him.

'It's mother and father.'

Bobby would drive her crazy with his inner-city accent. She spoke properly, according to herself.

The people in the inner city were poor. Bobby and Jay felt rich. They always had money and went to places none of their friends did. Anto had taken them to see Barry McGuigan fight. The tickets were fifty pounds each. They had been to see Ireland beat Malta 8–0. Bobby could remember Liam Brady's goals clearer than any of the others. When he got the ball at his feet, he was a magician; he was the master, he was the best Irish football player ever. Bobby loved the ease with which he strolled around the pitch. He walked with his shoulders hunched forward and he looked lazy, but nobody could get the ball from him.

Bobby loved Italy the most. He had been excited for weeks about going to see them play Ireland in

Dalymount Park. He still copied Marco Tardelli's celebration from the World Cup final in 1982. He scored in the second half to win the World Cup for Italy. After the ball hit the back of the net, Tardelli jumped off the ground and ran around like a lunatic, shaking his arms down by his side. He had veins the size of small rivers running down his arms. Bobby tried shaking his arms like Tardelli, but no veins ever appeared.

Anto had really bad scarring from burns he got in the Stardust disco in 1981. Forty-eight young people died at the disco. Anto never talked about it, but everyone in Ballybough knew his arms had been burned when he was trying to save people. Jay's mam said he ran back into the burning building to pull people out of the fire, and that he had saved many lives. The scars didn't take away any of his strength.

They always stood in the same spot in Daly-mount Park. And they always got in the same way. Anto wasn't scabby, he just refused to pay into Dalymount. He saw it as his mission to bonk in, with Bobby and Jay always in tow. There were always a few hundred people who tried to bonk in. Anto was the master bonker inner. He could get them over the wall in seconds. The plan, if a security guard saw them, was to scarper in separate directions and meet at their spot behind the goal.

When they arrived at Dalymount, there were thousands of people all trying to get in through three small turnstiles. There were also thousands of people trying to get down the bonker inner lane.

'There's no way we'll get in there, there's too many people,' said Anto.

Anto spotted a few people climbing over a gate that led into a truck yard behind the stand.

'Why don't we follow them over the gate?' said Jay seriously.

'It's too dangerous,' said Anto.

'We could climb over that easily,' said Bobby.

'Are you sure?' said Anto, staring at them to see if there was any fear in their eyes.

'You'll be the one struggling to get over it,' laughed Jay.

Climbing gates was easy for them. If your foot was small enough you could wedge it between the side of the gate and the wall. Bobby took a size three. Jay took a four. Anto's foot was much bigger, but he was able to use his strength to get up the gate quicker than any of the others. Bobby loved the excitement of bonking in; it was the same adrenalin rush that boxing and running gave him. When Bobby got to the top of the wall, he couldn't believe how many people were in the ground. The terrace was jam-packed. He held on to the top of the wall with his hands and let go. He hit the ground with a thump.

'We'll make it down to the front lads, follow me. It's too dangerous to try and get our normal spot.'

Anto led the way, followed by Jay and Bobby. There was an Ireland flag on a big pole directly in front of them. About halfway down, there was a sudden surge from behind. Bobby felt himself being lifted off the ground. He looked down at his feet dangling and when he looked up, he had lost Anto and Jay. He had no control over where he was moving. He started shouting as loud as he could for Anto and Jay. Bobby couldn't see anything. All he could see was the parka jacket of the person in front of him. His face was right up against it. There was no room for him to move. He had to turn his head sideways as it was getting more and more difficult to catch a breath. He thought about trying to get down onto the ground, but then it occurred to him that he might get trampled on. He tried to scream Anto's name as loud as he could, but he felt like he was wasting valuable energy. He thought he was going to die. It started to hurt his chest to try and take a breath. Then he spotted one of the crush barriers that people leaned against.

'If I can get to that…' thought Bobby.

He wriggled and wriggled until he felt his feet touch the ground. He reached out and grabbed at the bottom of the metal barrier. He forced himself through a sea of legs to a tiny spot directly underneath, where nobody could stand. He waited until he got his breath back and then screamed Anto's name as loud as he could over and over again. He knew there was no way Anto was going to hear his name through the sea of bodies. He could feel the tears welling up in his eyes. The legs around him seemed to be getting closer and closer. He was beginning to feel uncomfortable and he needed to pee. Then the urge took over and he peed in his pants. He couldn't stop it.

He closed his eyes and thought about Jay. Where was Jay? What if he hadn't made it to safety? He had just resigned himself to being in that tiny spot sitting in his own pee for the next two hours when he heard his name. It got louder and louder over the hum of the crowd. He looked around at all the shoes. Then he spotted a new pair of Nike runners moving against the tide of old shoes. Anto always had new Nike runners and kept them spotless. Bobby screamed his name. He could see the runners getting closer. Anto was weaving around bodies quicker than Bobby dribbled around cones at training. Bobby reached out and grabbed Anto's ankle. Anto reached down and grabbed Bobby's hand. Bobby felt like Anto was going to break it he was gripping it so tight.

'Are you OK?'

'Yeah,' Bobby said, holding the tears in.

He had felt closer to death in the crush than he

ever had before. There was a panic and a sick feeling inside him. There was no eerie calm.

'Where is Jay?'

Anto lifted Bobby up by the armpits.

'Can you see him? He should be straight ahead.'

Bobby spotted Jay, clinging to the railings behind the goal. He was holding on with one arm, while looking back up the terrace.

'Jay! Jay!' he shouted, waving both hands in the air.

Jay saw him and waved back. He was shouting, but Bobby couldn't hear what he was saying. Anto had to force his way down the terrace. Bobby knew that when he had kids, he would be taking them to Dalymount and to Tolka Park to see Ireland play, crush or no crush. His dad preferred the pub to football matches, even though he loved football. Bobby would never choose the pub over a football match.

'Make sure you don't let go,' Anto ordered.

Bobby held on tighter than he had ever held on to anyone's hand in his life. Anto said 'excuse me' hundreds of times as he pushed by the people on the terrace. Bobby knew he would be safe. Anto lifted Jay down and moved them to the corner of the pitch.

'What happened your trousers?'

'Someone spilt a can on me in the crush,' Bobby lied

Anto was charming enough to the man on the gate for him to let them get onto the side of the pitch. It was much safer there. Eventually the man had to let hundreds of other people onto the pitch to avoid the crush. Bobby and Jay were delighted. They were standing on the sideline, within touching distance of the players. Just before Paolo Rossi scored the first goal, the ball came out of play and Anto picked it up. Rossi ran over to take the throw-in. Anto handed Bobby the ball.

'You give it to him.'

Bobby threw Rossi the ball. He caught it and said something in Italian to Bobby, but Bobby couldn't understand.

'No problemo,' Bobby said back to him.

Rossi was the top scorer in the 1982 World Cup. Bobby couldn't believe he had just thrown him a football. He was much smaller in real life than he looked on television. From Uruguay in 1930, to Italy in 1982, Bobby knew all the winners and the score in each World Cup final. His favourite was the 1978 final in Argentina. Mario Kempes, with his long flowing locks, scored in the final when the pitch was covered in confetti. There was more white confetti than green grass to be seen. The Argentinians won the World Cup for the first time and Holland had lost the final for a second time in a row. That final was in Buenos Aires. The attendance was eighty thousand. The Argentinians went mad.

So did the crowd that night when Gary Waddock scored for Ireland. He got the ball at the far end of the pitch from Bobby. Just on the edge of the box. Took it down with his thigh and buried it in the bottom left-hand corner. The net rustled and the crowd went mad, shouting 'Gary, Gary, Gary' and 'Come on you boys in green'. The atmosphere was electric. Bobby knew the hairs on the back of your neck were supposed to stand up. He wasn't old enough to have hairs on his neck, and if they ever grew he would shave them off. He hated standing beside an old man at a match if he had a hairy neck; a hairy neck usually meant a blackhead-infested neck.

Bobby was good at estimating crowds; every match had an announcement of the official attendance. The unofficial attendance would include the bonker-inners. He reckoned there were at least forty thousand people watching the world champions beat Ireland 2–1 that night.

'And the official attendance for tonight's game is twenty-five thousand.'

The announcement made the whole crowd laugh, because they all knew they couldn't announce that there were fifteen thousand people clever enough to bonk in. It was the biggest crush Bobby had ever experienced, much worse than Croke Park on All-Ireland final day.

It was an amazing Wednesday night in Dublin,

even with the fear that he was going to be crushed. Walking back from Dalyer that night, Bobby wanted to call in to the Sunset House to tell his dad about the game.

'Don't say anything about the crush, he might not let you go to another match,' said Anto.

Bobby ran in on his own, excited out of his mind about the match. The crush wasn't important; being there was.

'What was the result, son?'

Bobby noticed the Guinness moustache his dad had.

'Italy won 2–1.'

'Ah,' he said after a big slug of Guinness, 'that's a pity.'

'It was brilliant though. Anto got us onto the side of the pitch. I gave the ball to Paolo Rossi.'

'That's great. Now run on home. It's too late for you to be in the pub.'

Bobby walked outside and could see Anto and Jay chatting in the distance. He sprinted as fast as he could to catch up. Anto walked Bobby home to his house.

'I heard on the radio there was a crush in the stadium where the Ireland match was being played,' said a worried Laura when she met them at the front door.

'Not in the part of the ground where we were, Mrs Ryan.'

Anto always had a quick answer to allay her fears. Bobby looked up at Anto, who gave him the smile. The smile that said it all.

CHAPTER 2

Bobby wasn't allowed to drink anything after six o'clock, but he still drank the can of Coke Anto had bought him on the way home from the match. If he was late for his dinner, he would have to have it with no liquid. He hated the rule, but if it stopped him wetting the bed, he would give it a try. He had tried everything else. His mother would wake him before she went to bed, to pee in a potty. His bladder produced world-record amounts of pee.

Kevin said he was afraid of heights. It wasn't a very long way down but Kevin constantly reminded Bobby that he was doing him a favour by sleeping on the top bunk.

'Do you want to sleep down here?'

'On your pissy bed? No thanks.'

'I gave the ball to Paolo Rossi.'

'Who the hell is he?'

'The best footballer in the world.'

Bobby put both his feet on the laths that held Kevin up and pushed as hard as he could.

'Piss off or I'll kill you.'

It would drive Kevin insane. He was much stronger than Bobby and could kill him. If he put him in a head lock, Bobby couldn't do anything about it. He had kicked Bobby twice in the head the previous Christmas and put him in hospital. Bobby couldn't even remember that he supported Liverpool. That's when his dad knew there was something seriously wrong with him. He had lost his memory. The doctors called it amnesia. Bobby couldn't hold a grudge, because he couldn't remember what had happened. He liked pushing his brother to the point where he would flip. Or the point just before that when he would be raging and on the verge of flipping. Anything could do it. He would say 'Dire Straits are shit' or 'Jimi Hendrix is crap at guitar' and it would drive him over the edge, to the point of no return.

Their room wasn't big enough to have both beds on the floor. There was a wardrobe in the corner beside the window and a dart board on the back of the door. Jay loved playing darts. He had his own board and was much better at darts than Bobby. Jay had never been in Bobby's bedroom. The reason Bobby gave was that his ma said nobody was allowed in the house. Bobby would imitate her saying, 'Play on the road, you're not allowed in the house.' Bobby knew Jay would smell pee in the room. He knew that's why his brother hated him too.

Both beds had orange mattresses. Bobby really wanted to have a non-pissy mattress. His was wrecked because of his world-record bladder. His mam told him there was no way of stopping it. And there was no point in buying a new mattress every few months. Doctors didn't know why people did it. They could give someone a heart transplant, but they couldn't fix Bobby's bladder. He knew there must be a reason why it happened.

If he was lucky there was one day each month when he didn't wet the bed. His mattress was now so badly damaged that his sheet had a black bin liner underneath to protect it. It worked. But when he did let loose during the night, a puddle would form in the middle of the bin liner. It was routine for Bobby by now.

Take the wet sheet off.
Carefully remove the black sack.
Take the potty out from under the bed.
Pour the black sack into the potty.
Turn the mattress.
Get back into bed.
Put the pillow at the opposite end.

He would try to sleep against the wall, because the sides of the mattress were the only parts that kept dry. It wasn't always easy to get back to sleep when you were hugging a cold wall. At times anything would have been better than lying in a bed of piss. His skin would be sticky and smelly. He wouldn't be able to sleep. He sometimes thought death would be better than waking up every morning covered in pee. He didn't think there were any piss-in-the-beds in heaven.

Bobby would be the first up every morning. He would go downstairs to the bathroom and run the water for a shallow bath. There was no hot water in the mornings, so it was a cold, shallow puddle he had to sit in. He scrubbed every inch of his body over and over in cold, soapy water with a scourer. He didn't care if it left red marks all over his skin, he was paranoid about smelling of pee.

There was no rule about drinking during the day.

'Let's see who can drink a litre the fastest,' said Jay.

They both ripped the top corner of the carton open.

'On your marks, get set, go!' said Bobby.

They gulped and gulped and gulped. Orange juice spilled down the sides of both their faces onto their T-shirts. Jay finished first. He was the champion gulper. Bobby never had the opportunity to drink as much orange juice as he wanted before. Normally it was one small glass for breakfast when he was lucky.

'Two down, twenty-two to go.'

It was their first time breaking into Goodall's Foods. Goodall's had premises beside the paper factory, which was on the banks of the Tolka River. A big, green, metal gate stopped people entering, but the gate had a thick plastic flap at the bottom.

'What do you think the flap is for, Jay?'

'I haven't got a clue.'

Jay got down on his hands and knees and looked under it.

'The smell is disgusting.'

'What can you see?'

'Metal shelves with all sorts of stuff on them. I can see red sauce, brown sauce and orange juice.'

By the time Jay got to 'orange juice', all Bobby could see were his legs. Bobby held on to his foot.

'You're not going any further.'

'OK, let go!'

Bobby released his grip and Jay disappeared under the gate. Bobby's heart was pounding. He got down to see what Jay was doing. As he did, a box of orange juice came out the flap, followed by another one.

'Hide them behind the pallets.'

Bobby hid the cartons of juice behind wooden pallets that were in the yard of the paper factory. They always had a huge stack of pallets. They were brilliant at Hallowe'en for the bonfire. And for leaning up against the trunk of a tree. If Bobby and Jay couldn't reach the first branch, they borrowed a pallet from the yard. It was a permanent borrow, but when there were hundreds against the wall, one or two wouldn't be missed.

Bobby got back to the flap and looked in. Jay was inspecting one of the metal shelves. Bobby could see that the shelves were in an open yard with the indoor part of the factory a little bit further back. Jay reached in to a shelf and lifted out a tray of red sauce. The bottles were red with a yellow label on them. The tray was sealed in plastic. Jay ripped it open and pulled out two bottles. He slid them along the ground to Bobby. Jay pulled out another two and put one in each pocket. He looked at Bobby and put his hands down by his side.

'Don't move,' said Jay.

He pulled the bottle of sauce out of his pocket like it was a gun, opened the cap and squirted it at Bobby. Bobby covered his head with his arm, and when he looked up, he could see a man in blue overalls approaching Jay. He was walking quietly. Bobby could see a smirk on his face.

'What do you think you're doing?' he roared, frightening the shit out of Jay. Bobby slid backwards and held the flap up. Jay came out head first with the bottle of sauce still in his hand.

'Leg it,' shouted Jay.

Bobby knew what 'leg it' meant. They were the words the sketch-keeper or look-out used when

they robbed orchards to alert the robber that someone was coming. It should have been Bobby saying
it to Jay but he couldn't get the words out. It
required nerves of steel to rob. Jay had them.
Bobby was always the sketch-keeper.

They ran through the yard of the paper factory,
up the hill at the back and into the grounds of Holy
Cross College. It was a training college for priests.
They must have spent all their time inside praying
and reading the Bible because Bobby and Jay never
saw any of them walking around the amazing
grounds. A narrow pathway with huge trees on
one side and the back wall of the paper factory on
the other led to the Tolka River, which ran all the
way along the back of the college.

Jay had his favourite horse chestnut tree for
climbing. When they got to it, Jay flew up, putting
his feet in exactly the same spot on each branch
that he had done hundreds of times previously.
Bobby followed, watching the soles of Jay's
runners getting further and further away, until he
dangled from the branch he always sat on. Jay was
laughing with excitement. Bobby was laughing
nervously, looking behind him to see if they were
being chased.

'Come on, slow coach!'

Bobby had heard that before. No matter how
hard he tried, he could never climb as quickly as
Jay. Bobby felt something cold hitting his head.

'A bird just shit on your head!'

Bobby didn't want to touch it, because he didn't want bird poo on his hand, and he didn't want to let go of the branch. He looked up at Jay, who had the red sauce pointing down. He was gently squeezing the bottle, letting one drop out at a time.

'Give it over!' squealed Bobby.

'You'll have red hair by the time you get up here if it takes you any longer.'

The two of them sat on the branch, looking back down the pathway. If anyone came after them, they were safe. They were invisible amongst the branches of the tree.

'Do you want to have a red-sauce fight?' asked Jay.

'Here?'

'No, beside the waterfall.'

'My mam will kill me if I come home covered in red sauce.'

'You won't get it on your clothes.'

'Just aiming at the head?'

'No, you dope, we'll take our clothes off. And then wash ourselves in the Tolka.'

Bobby loved getting into the Tolka, even though it was freezing. At the top of the waterfall, the water was perfectly calm and clear. Every other part of it looked as filthy as it was. They covered each other in red sauce. Bobby didn't try to escape from the squirts and neither did Jay. When the sauce ran out, they dived into the water to clean themselves. They ducked themselves under the water and had swimming races, which Jay always won no matter how much of a head start he gave Bobby.

They had orange-juice drinking competitions every day for the next week, even though the juice became more disgusting the longer it stayed behind the pallets. It made them feel sick, but they had fun feeling sick.

Bobby couldn't always swim. He had nearly drowned when he played for the Ballybough United under tens. They were playing a night of indoor matches against the boys from the School for the Blind. All the Ballybough United lads thought this was hilarious. How could they see the ball? See it they did. And they also heard it. The ball they played with had what sounded like bells inside it. Bobby had never played against a team as aggressive as the blind boys. It was like they had something to prove. The minute the whistle went, they kicked lumps out of the Ballybough boys. They won four out of the five games.

The School for the Blind had a swimming pool as well as an indoor gym. The dressing-rooms were four times as big as the ones in Sean MacDermott Street swimming pool. And they were clean. Sean Mac was verruca city. A killer verruca meant no football. Jay got a disgusting verruca when he was ten. It took over the whole sole of his foot. Jay would pick at the skin and throw it at Bobby.

Most of the lads were already on a huge floating tube when Bobby took his two tiptoe steps through the cloudy, shallow, disgusting, disinfected pool. He hated it touching his feet. He tried to jump over it one day and wrecked himself. He ran and jumped straight on top of the tube, knocking Jay off as he landed. Jay swam to the side and climbed out of the pool. He launched himself at the tube, landing in the middle. Bobby got splashed in the face but managed to cling on. One of the strong lads from the Blind team was next to launch. He was twice the size of Bobby. As Bobby thought he was going to get squashed, he let go, thinking his feet were inches from the bottom. He was in the deep end. He sank straight to the bottom. He could see four pairs of legs dangling from the tube. He pushed himself off the bottom and when his head hit the air, he took a deep breath and sank again. Bobby hadn't even learned how to tread water. From the bottom, he could see someone crash onto the tube. He pushed himself up again, this time slightly sideways. He took another big breath in, sank again, and repeated the sideways push up six more times before he made it to the side of the pool. He clung on there for what seemed like an eternity before making his way to the empty shallow end. It was the first time he realised what could happen if you couldn't swim. He had never been in the deep end in Sean Mac when he was ten. He had been in the Irish Sea a few times when he was younger, but just to paddle. He stayed in the shallow end looking at all the swimmers having the best time of their lives. Jay hadn't even noticed. Bobby was determined to learn how to swim. He told Jay on the way home what had happened.

'I'll teach you how to swim.'

'Do you think I'll be able?'

'It's easy, you won't drown in the shallow end of Sean Mac.'

Over the next few weeks, Jay taught Bobby how to swim. He wasn't as good as Jay, but he could swim. That was all he needed. He knew he would never be afraid of drowning again.

Bobby thought about death a lot. He knew what suicide was. He had heard about people hanging themselves and sticking their heads in gas ovens. The thought entered his head sometimes as to what would happen if he walked in front of the number 23 bus. He knew he would die, but what happened next is what he thought about. Some people had thrown themselves into the River Liffey and drowned. He never thought about doing that. He didn't want to die when he was on the bottom of the deep end, but an eerie calm had come over him. He knew everything was going to be all right. He didn't know if Jay thought about death like he did. He was afraid to ask. It was a secret he had to keep to himself. So was wetting the bed. If he didn't wet the bed, maybe he wouldn't think about death any more.

CHAPTER 3

Bobby was surrounded by old people. His neighbours on one side were a couple in their seventies called Eileen and Ned. They had a dog called Smartie who made it his mission in life to jump over the back wall into Croke Park. The wall was seven feet high. He would jump up continuously for five minutes and then take a break, panting at a hundred miles an hour while he lay on the ground. When his breathing became slower and his tongue went back in his mouth, he would start jumping again. Then he would do it again, and again, all day long. Bobby had seen him cling to the top of the wall twice. He barely managed to glance at the freedom on offer before he slid back down into his small yard. Eileen said Smartie had bad hips. It didn't matter what you said back to her as she was stone deaf.

His other neighbour was Michael Dunne. He was ninety-six. He drank a naggin of whiskey every day, except Sundays when he drank two. Bobby couldn't understand why he didn't buy a large bottle as it would save him a fortune. Bobby would be sent to the Vine Tree off-licence on Bally-bough Road to make the purchase. He was allowed keep the two pence change, out of which he would buy two penny golfball chewing gums.

The Vine Tree's busiest day was when the Dubs played in Croke Park. Dublin's Gaelic football fans were either normal people or skinheads. The skinheads drank flagons of cider before matches. They hung around on the street outside Bobby's house, smoking cigarettes, singing songs and pissing up against the walls of the houses. Nobody said anything to them because they were skinheads; you didn't mess with skinheads. Some of them had the word 'skinhead' tattooed on their lips. Others had spiders' webs tattooed on their heads. One really fat skinhead had a shrine for every year Dublin won the All-Ireland tattooed on his back. 1891, 1892 … all the way to 1983. Bobby knew he would be getting 1985 on his back in a few months' time. Barney Rock was on fire and Dublin would get their revenge on Kerry for defeat in the 1984 semi-final.

Every Saturday morning Anto brought Bobby and Jay on a sixty-minute run. Out past Fairview Park and along the coast road to Clontarf and the wooden bridge that Bobby always thought was going to collapse. Jay would bounce up and down, holding on to the side of the bridge, trying to make it shake. It would give Bobby a horrible, nervous knot in his stomach.

'Running is great for the cardiovascular system,' Bobby would explain.'

'The what?' asked Jay.

'The heart.'

'Then why didn't you just say that?'

'Because that's what it's called.'

Anto liked the quiet and breathing in the sea air as he ran.

'I'm sick of listening to the two of you, will you shut up and concentrate.'

Anto knew how to shut them up. He would pick up the pace of the run to a point where they were just about hanging on and unable to speak.

'I'm moving into a house on Foster Terrace. It's number 8, four houses down from Ballybough Road,' announced Anto. 'Call over when you get back.'

Anto sprinted away from the two of them with a few miles left. Bobby stared at the size of the muscles in his legs as he disappeared into the distance.

Foster Terrace was parallel to Sackville Avenue. Ardilaun Road, where Bobby lived, joined the two roads together.

'I'll need a hand moving some of my stuff. The garden is in bits too, so I'll have some work for the two of you.'

'Now Jay will call you a poshie!'

Jay would slag Bobby, saying he was a poshie because he lived in a house. He couldn't have really meant it, because his flat was bigger than Bobby's house, and his mam worked and was on the social welfare, whereas Bobby's dad was just on the social welfare. Bobby hated it when he called him a poshie. Kevin was a poshie. He had oxblood Doc Martens and a fringe. The one thing Bobby didn't want to be was a poshie. He wanted to be a Ballybough boy, just like Jay.

Bobby's mam said that the people in the flats were different. Bobby didn't think they were different, he wanted to be like the people in the flats. He thought all people were the same. Some just had more money than others.

From the front balcony of Anto's house you could see the houses on Foster Terrace, and all the way down Ballybough Road to the Tolka River. You could see four of the seven pubs in Ballybough from the front balcony and the other three from the back. That was an average of one pub every one hundred metres.

Inside the house, Anto had all his stuff in boxes. One was marked 'Boxing Videos'.

'How many boxing videos have you got?' asked Bobby.

'So many I've lost count. I have all the classic fights.'

Bobby didn't have a video recorder. Neither did Jay.

'Can we watch a few of them?'

'You can watch them all if you get these boxes around to the house and bring this video up to a friend of mine.'

Anto handed them a video with the *Thriller in Manila* written on the side. It was in a snap-shut box and had a picture of Ali with the world title belt on the front and back.

'Here you go. Johnny is another boxing fan. He lives in number 19 in the Strand flats.'

Bobby hated everything about the Strand flats. It was rival territory. He felt safe in Ballybough flats. Jay was fearless and Bobby kept his agitation to himself. The stairwells were the same as Ballybough flats. They had the same smell. It was a lingering smell of urine, mixed with boiled cabbage and the rubbish bins that overflowed from the shop at the entrance to the stairs.

Bobby couldn't understand why people would pee in their own stairwells. Or throw bags of rubbish on the ground outside their front door. The smell in one stairwell of the Strand flats was smellier than all the stairwells put together in Ballybough flats.

There were forty-two steps to get to the top. Each

step was eighteen inches wide on the left-hand side going up and two inches wide on the left hand side coming down. Bobby and Jay never walked up or down the stairwells. They would sprint flat out to limit the amount of toxic fumes going up their nostrils.

Number 19 had a yellow door, with no knocker or bell. It used to have two frosted glass panes, but now it had plywood nailed on from the inside. The remnants of the old glass pane were sticking up from the corner of the window frame.

Jay gave a loud knock on the plywood. Johnny answered the door. Shirtless and skinny.

'Howyis lads, me oul friend Anto is a good lad. What video did he send you up with?'

'The *Thriller in Manila*,' said Bobby.

'Ah, great, Cassius Clay and George Foreman, lovely stuff, happy days. Tell me oul friend Anto I'll see him later. Nice one, nice one.'

The door closed and Bobby looked at Jay.

'Last one down is a bag of shit.'

The two of them took off down the stairs, Bobby just ahead of Jay. They got about half way down and flew around the constant bend, swerving to avoid somebody on the way up. Bobby stopped to apologise, and Jay kept going, shouting 'bag of shit' as he passed. Bobby turned to say sorry and realised it was Angela.

'Eh, he wasn't calling you a bag of shit, we were

racing down and last one down was a bag of shit.'

'You are the bag of shit, so,' smiled Angela.

Bobby couldn't take his eyes off her.

'Are you all right, you bag of shit?' shouted Jay from the bottom.

'You'd better go.'

'OK, see ya.'

Bobby turned to walk away and glanced behind to get one last glimpse. Angela turned at the same time and smiled.

'What were you doing up there?'

'I told Angela you fancied her, she is going to call over to you later.'

'Yeah, right.'

'She's not bad though, is she?' asked Bobby, not knowing what Jay's response would be.

'Not bad for a nig...nig... Ballybough girl!'

Jay would never call her a nigger. She was the only black girl in Ballybough. He knew Bobby fancied her. Bobby knew Jay did, too. She was so beautiful that Bobby could never imagine her fancying him. He had never kissed a girl. His brother had. He had overheard Kevin talking to his friend about kissing a girl called Cheryl at a school disco. Bobby was too young to go to a school disco. He kissed his pillow at night pretending it was Angela. He knew you were supposed to use your tongue, but he didn't know what you were supposed to do with it. The pillow was too dry to lick, so he just tipped his tongue off it instead.

It was a really short walk up the avenue and down the four doors to Anto's new house. Jay took the key out and opened the door. They put the first two boxes in the living room at the front of the house and made seven journeys up and down the avenue, carrying Anto's belongings. He let them watch Ali v Frazier when they were finished their work. It wasn't an original. Anto had a way of copying videos: he had two video recorders and he hired all the boxing videos he could find. And he copied and sold them. Ali v Frazier was his favourite. They had fought each other before, but the *Thriller in Manila* was their last, brutal fight. President Marcos of the Philippines had paid them millions of dollars to bring the fight to his country. And, because of time-zone differences, it had to be staged at the hottest part of a sweltering day, so that viewers in America could watch the fight live. Anto told them all the details before leaving them to watch the fourteen rounds. He was an encyclopaedia on boxing. Jay and Bobby were transfixed by the brutality. Ali and Frazier had once been friends. Frazier had given Ali money when he was banned from boxing for refusing to fight in the Vietnam War. In the build-up to their fight in the Philippines, Ali had goaded Frazier, calling him a gorilla and an Uncle Tom. Bobby didn't know what an Uncle Tom was.

'Did you like the fight?' asked Anto.

'It was amazing, how many more have you got?'

'I have them all.'

Anto gave them a fiver each for their two hours' work.

'That won't be the end of it lads, if you're interested in more work around the house. I'm going to paint it and gut the garden. There'll be a lot more fivers. It'll be great exercise too.'

Bobby and Jay were delighted. A fiver was a lot of money. Bobby only got twenty-five pence for his pocket money. He didn't tell his mam. He knew she'd say 'that's too much money'. Bobby's dad used to have a car, but he had amassed a thousand pounds in parking fines and had received a two-year driving ban for another traffic offence. Bobby didn't know what the offence was. His dad didn't believe in using parking meters or in reading the fine that would appear on the window as a result. He was eventually summonsed to court, where he agreed to pay a fiver a week to the parking fines man, who would always call to the house on a Friday evening around seven o'clock. Bobby's mam either took a fiver out of her purse to give to Bobby for him, or he was told to say that there was nobody home. Bobby knew that, at five pounds a week, the man would be calling for a long time. In one hundred weeks, he would have handed over five hundred, so it would take two hundred weeks to pay off the fines. Nearly four years. He had heard a row one Friday night after his dad came home from the Sunset. Bobby had been told to say his dad wasn't in when the fines' man called. His mam was shouting at him that if they didn't pay the fines, he would end up in prison. He didn't go to the Sunset the next Friday. The fines man got paid. When he had sold the car after the driving ban, he had got fifty pounds for it. It was a Morris Traveller and a banger. Bobby was embarrassed getting into it. The floors in the back had holes in them, so if you sat in there you had to be careful your feet didn't touch the road as the car was moving.

CHAPTER 4

'I'll have the seven bananas for a pound special please.'

'Here you go, love.'

Bernie put the fruit in a plastic bag and handed it to the customer. The young woman opened the bag and took out one of the bananas. It had black spots on it. It was very ripe. Bobby hated them with black spots. He preferred them a little bit green. They were a bit drier and didn't have as much of a banana taste off them. He couldn't eat them at all if they had a black spot on the inside of them.

'Can I have the greener ones instead, please?' asked the woman.

Bobby knew what she meant. The ones she had been given would be too ripe within hours.

'If you want to choose them yourself, it's only five for a pound.'

'That's ridiculous.'

'That's the way it is, if you don't like it you can go somewhere else.'

The fruit sellers were like actresses and Bernie was queen amongst them. Her mother had been a fruit seller before her. They were constantly putting on a show. They would always be gathered in groups of two or three, and when anyone stopped at their stall they would invariably say, 'Do you want something, love?' like you were interrupting a good chat. They never had lessons in customer service; they made up the rules themselves. One side of Moore Street had fruit sellers; the other side had fish sellers. The smell on the street was horrible. On a summer's day there would be loads of bluebottles flying around the fish. The sellers just laid the fish out on their tables. Flies or not, people still bought the fish. Molly Malone had sold cockles and mussels on Moore Street. It was mainly cod and whiting now, with the odd bluebottle thrown in for free. Bobby had never seen a cockle or a mussel.

The city centre was a ten-minute walk from Ballybough. There was a brand-new shopping centre built beside where Jay's ma worked her stall. The people at the Ilac Centre thought it would be a good idea to put a fountain in the middle of it where people could throw their pennies. Jay thought it was a good idea too. He had longer arms than Bobby and could reach in farther. The security guard caught them one day and kicked them out. Not before Jay got fourteen pennies. They bought two JR ice pops and licked them all the way home. The fountain was eventually emptied of water because there were loads of people stealing the pennies.

'Come on into Dunnes Stores and I'll show you the jeans.'

When they did go into the shops in town, they would be followed by security, or not let in. Bobby knew it was because they were inner-city boys. Some shops were more security conscious than others. Jay decided he wanted to buy a new pair of jeans with the money they were getting from Anto. And if Jay wanted a pair, then Bobby had to have a pair too.

The two of them went in and didn't get followed. The jeans were on the second floor of Dunnes. An escalator took them up. They walked past the shoes and jumpers and there they were. About ten different types of jeans to choose from.

Bobby picked up a pair of light blue jeans that had a dark blue line running down the side. It was barely visible.

'What do you think of these, Jay?'

'Not bad, try them on.'

'No, this is my size. I don't need to try them on.'

'Don't be stupid, try them on, I'm going to try on this black pair.'

'They are twenty pounds.'

'So?'

'You haven't got twenty pounds.'

'I'm only trying them on.'

Bobby's jeans were so tight at the bottom that he nearly lost his balance and fell through the curtain trying to get them off. The new jeans slipped on easily. He looked in the mirror and thought the jeans looked good. He pulled back the curtain to show Jay.

'What do you think?'

'You're gorgeous, Angela will be chasing you later.'

'Yeah, right.'

'She'll knock you out with her basketballs.'

'Are you getting the black ones?'

'Nope, I just wanted to see what they look like. Hurry up.'

Bobby could hear Jay laughing at him trying to get the tight jeans back on.

'Have those jeans got holes to put your feet through?'

Bobby came out, jeans in hand.

'Leave them there, we have to go.'

'Why?'

'Questions later.'

Jay started walking more briskly than normal.

'What's the story?'

'I'll tell you in a minute.'

'I wanted to buy those jeans.'

'I bought the black ones.'

'What?'

Jay pulled out the waist of his tracksuit bottoms. Bobby could see the black jeans underneath.

'You're a fucking lunatic. Why didn't you tell me you were going to do that?'

'Because you would have tried to stop me.'

'You have the money to buy a pair.'

'Not these ones. The buzz is in robbing them. Do you think you could do it?'

'Why would I do it when I can buy them? My ma would kill me if she found out.'

'That's because you're a poshie.'

'Piss off, how am I a poshie?'

'Your ma is posh and your brother goes to school in Clontarf.'

'She's not posh. And my dad is on the social welfare.'

'Yeah, right.'

'I bet your ma makes more money than my dad ever will.'

They walked in silence until they got to Barney's amusement arcade. Bobby thought it would be better to be called a piss-in-the-bed than a poshie. All he wanted was to be the same as Jay. He robbed orchards and bonked in to Croker. They had squirted each other with red sauce. They had been in every derelict house in Ballybough snaring pigeons with their bare hands. Jay's flat was bigger than Bobby's house. Jay was his best friend. He had never slagged Jay about his da being in prison. Bobby felt betrayed. Maybe he *was* different. He couldn't concentrate on playing Mario Brothers.

'I'm going to the bookies. Are you coming?'

'No, poshie.'

Bobby walked out of the amusement arcade with his head feeling fuzzy. He never fought with Jay and it made him feel sick. He thought about going back to Dunnes to rob a pair of jeans. He thought about what would happen if Jay didn't want to be friends with him. He was the best friend Bobby could ever have. He walked into Ladbrokes and stared at the *Sporting Life*. The early afternoon always had loads of greyhound races on. The voice came over the tannoy to announce the starting prices for the 1.33 at Catford. The man wrote them onto a board with his black marker. Trap two was 2–1 favourite. It had won its last four races.

'Put it on trap two.'

Bobby turned around to see Jay smiling at him.

'I was thinking trap two.'

Bobby took out a docket and picked up a bookie's pencil. He wrote *£1 win T-2 1:33 Catford* on the docket.

'That is one pound and ten pence, please.'

The hare is running at Catford.

A race only lasted about thirty seconds. If the dog got to the first bend in the lead, it had a good chance of winning. If it was last to the first bend, you could tear up your docket. The voice came over the tannoy again with the commentary for the race. Trap 2 was last out of the traps. Bobby thought his trap was spiked with a tin of Pedigree Chum. The race was over before it started, unless the other five dogs collapsed.

Trap six wins, second is trap three, and the dog with the red jacket, trap one, is third. Close for fourth between five and four. Trap two trails in last.

If Bobby didn't make it as a boxer, he wanted to be a tannoy announcer in Ladbrokes.

'How much did you lose?'

'Only a pound.'

Bobby didn't care about losing the bet. Jay was back by his side. He had only been gone for a few minutes and Bobby had thought it could be forever.

'Why do you do bets?'

'For the buzz.'

'The buzz is the reason I robbed the jeans.'

'So I have my buzz and you have yours.'

'We are buzz brothers,' laughed Jay.

They walked back to Ballybough as buzz brothers. Bobby was glad Jay had followed him. He hated that Jay slagged him about being a poshie, but he loved the fact that the fight with Jay had only lasted for five minutes.

CHAPTER 5

There were cans of Coke, Pepsi and Club Orange in the fridge in Anto's house. He gave Bobby and Jay permission to drink as many as they wanted while they were helping him clear his garden of the weeds and overgrown bushes. At the back of his garden was a row of evergreen trees. Two wood pigeons lived in one of them. They were very fat, nearly too fat to fly. Bobby and Jay would dig for an hour, and then have a can; Bobby always had a Coke, Jay a Pepsi. He would goad Bobby that it was nicer, or that Bobby couldn't tell the difference between the two.

'I'll close my eyes and taste the two, I bet you ten pence I can tell the difference.'

'Ten pence! Is that all you've got?'

Jay held his hand over Bobby's eyes and gave him the first can, which was the Pepsi.

'That is deffo the Pepsi.'

Jay put the can down and picked up the same one again. Bobby took a sip.

'That's the Pepsi too, you bollox!'

'No it's not, I knew you couldn't tell the

difference. That's ten pence for me. You're working for free today.'

'You gave me the Pepsi twice, I'm not stupid.'

'Progress is very slow lads, drop this video up to Johnny to earn your fiver today,' said Anto.

'Johnny, the boxing expert.'

'Is he a boxing expert?' asked Anto.

'He thought George Foreman fought in the *Thriller in Manila*,' said Jay.

'I'd better give him the *Rumble in the Jungle*, so.'

Anto went to his room and came out with the *Rumble* video tape.

'Here you go. Drop this up and I'll give you a fiver each when you get back.'

They headed up to Johnny's flat and had a race up the stairs, which Jay claimed he won. Just as they got to his flat, the door opened and Gringo walked out. He was the most feared lad in the Strand flats. He had a shaven head and huge ears. They called him Fa because his ears looked like the handles on the FA Cup. He walked by them and Johnny came out onto the landing.

'Lads, how are me oul flowers?'

'We're grand, what did you think of the last video?'

'Yeah it was great, which one was it again?'

'The *Thriller in the Jungle*,' said Bobby.

'Brilliant, it was brilliant. What have you got for me today?'

'The *Rumble in Manila*,' said Jay.

'Brilliant, tell Anto thanks a million.'

Johnny took the video and closed the door. Bobby looked at Jay and said, 'Mad fucker.'

'Mad bastard,' Jay responded. 'Last one down is Johnny in disguise.'

They took off down the landing, pushing each other as they turned into the top of the stairwell. Standing on the top step was Gringo. He had his arms out.

'Stop there lads.'

They came to a grinding halt.

'Empty your pockets.'

Bobby felt like he was going to poo in his pants. It was an involuntary muscle movement he had never felt before. One second he was fine, the next he needed to poo worse than ever before. Bobby took out some change. Jay had a five-pound note and some coins.

'Is that all you've got?' Gringo roared in Bobby's face.

'Yeah.'

Gringo took it and ran off down the stairwell.

'What are we going to do?' asked Bobby.

'We have to tell Anto.'

They walked to the bottom of the stairwell without racing or talking. Bobby's hands were shaking. He put them in his pockets so Jay wouldn't see.

'What a wanker. My hands are shaking,' said Jay.

'So are mine. Look.'

Bobby held out his hands to show Jay.

'Let's go tell Anto,' said Jay. 'That fucker is not going to get away with it.'

'He might never get us to do any jobs for him any more.'

'We're telling him.'

They strolled back down to Foster Terrace. Anto could tell something had happened.

'Is everything all right?'

'A fella called Gringo robbed our money at the top of the stairwell,' said Jay.

'Gringo. Is that his real name?'

'No, it's Steven Hart,' said Jay.

Bobby looked at him, puzzlingly.

'He was in Johnny's flat before we got there.'

'The little prick.'

Bobby had never heard Anto use bad language. Anto picked up the phone and dialled Johnny's number.

'Johnny, Anto here. Do you know a fella called Gringo? Or Steven Hart or something. Find him and have him in your flat in fifteen minutes.'

Anto nearly knocked the door off the hinges when they got to Johnny's flat. He banged repeatedly on the plywood window until the door opened.

'Is he here?'

'Yeah.'

There was a couch against one wall and a TV against another. The curtains were pulled across, blocking any light coming in from the balcony. Gringo was sitting on a chair. Anto walked up to him, grabbed him by the throat, lifted him up and pushed him against the wall. Bobby thought Anto's arms looked like melted plastic.

'If you ever lay a hand on the two of these boys again, I'll kill you. Do you understand me?'

Gringo couldn't answer, because Anto was choking him.

'How much did he take, lads?'

'About six quid.'

'How much have you got, fuck face?'

Anto released his grip and let Gringo look in his pockets for money. He took out a lighter, a box of John Player Blue, a packet of Rizla and some change.

'I would strongly advise you to take out some notes.'

Anto picked him up while still choking him, and brought him out onto the balcony. He leaned his head over the side.

'Do you want to find yourself flying off this balcony?'

Gringo reached into his back pocket and took out the five-pound note. He handed it to Anto, who turned to Johnny.

'Very bad company you're keeping, Johnny.

These lads are like brothers to me. And for their trouble I think they deserve more than their six quid. More like twenty quid.'

'OK, no problem.'

Johnny reached down the back of his stinky couch and pulled out a cigarette box. He opened it and pulled out a roll of notes. There was much more than twenty quid.

'Here.'

'It's not for me, give it to them.'

'Here you go, sorry about that; it will never happen again.'

'Make it a score each, Johnny.'

'Twenty quid each?'

'Is there a problem?'

'There's no problem,' said Johnny, frantically trying to unravel the notes.

Jay took the money and put it in his pocket. Bobby took his twenty-pound note and scrunched it up in his hand.

'Let's go,' said Anto, who was staring menacingly at Gringo as if to say, 'You were lucky this time'.

They walked out the door into the hall. Anto turned back to Johnny.

'I'll be seeing you later. Do you understand me?'

The boys didn't know what to say. They had never seen Anto get aggressive with anyone. He had seriously put the shits up Gringo, who was supposed to be the hardest lad in the Strand flats.

'He had loads of money in that box, Anto,' said Jay.

'The poor fucker has more money than sense. If anyone ever gives you any grief, you tell me and I'll sort it out.'

'OK, of course we will.'

'I'll see the two of you later at boxing.'

Bobby and Jay walked back to the flats. Bobby still had the twenty in his hand.

'What did you make of Anto?' asked Jay.

'More like what did you make of Gringo. I'd say he shit his pants when Anto dragged him out onto the balcony!'

They laughed and laughed at the thought of Gringo shitting in his pants.

Without fail the same time every Friday, the parking fines man knocked on the door. Just as *A Question of Sport* started on BBC1, the knock would come on the door.

'Tell him I'll pay him next week, Kevin,' said his mam.

Bobby jumped up from his favourite television programme.

'I'll tell him.'

'My mam gave me this to give to you,' Bobby whispered.

'Twenty pounds. Thanks a million.'

He wrote out the receipt and gave it to Bobby. Bobby put it in his pocket.

'See you next week.'

Bobby thought he may as well give the money to the parking fines man. After all, it wasn't his to begin with, and his dad was in the Sunset again.

'What did he say, Bobby?'

'He just said he'd call back next week.'

'Is that all he said? Did he look annoyed?'

'No, he was grand.'

Bobby went up to his room with the receipt. The carpet in his room was actually a rug over a carpet. The original carpet was a horrible brown colour. The new rug was red and really soft on your feet. The side of it had white tassels. Bobby pulled the rug back in the corner of his room. He put the receipt underneath. It was the same hiding place he had used before for his dad's cigarettes. His dad said he only smoked one pack of twenty a day. Bobby thought if he robbed three or four a day, and his dad didn't notice, then he would smoke less without realising. His granny and granddad had both died from smoking cigarettes and Bobby really wanted his dad to give up. He wrapped the borrowed cigarettes in tin foil and put them under the rug. After a week, he had twenty cigarettes. He took one of his dad's empty boxes and filled it up. He did the same for the next few weeks and gave them to his dad as a present. He thought his dad would be delighted.

'Sure, they're all stale now.'

'If they were dipped in Guinness you'd smoke them.'

'Get up to your room.'

That was the worst punishment Bobby could get.

CHAPTER 6

The unknown man had the shortest stay of any-body in the history of Ballybough. He moved into one of the bungalows on Sackville Avenue opposite the flats. Most of the bungalows were boarded up. The unknown man moved in on a Friday and moved out on a Sunday.

Git and Willo Brown used to be good at foot-ball. They played with Anto when he was younger.

'Stay away from them,' Anto would say.

They thought they were hard. Only because they had their father, Billy, to back them up. Billy Brown was hard. Bobby's dad said he was 'as hard as nails'. To annoy their new neighbour, the two Browns decided to kick a football up against his house. When he came out to tell them to stop, they would smile at him and say sorry. The second the hall door closed, they would start again. The enraged unknown man ran out with a long knife and the two Browns scarpered. He picked up the ball and rammed the knife straight through it. He had never met Billy Brown before.

Git and Willo ran up to their flat with the burst ball. Mr Brown came down, followed by his two daughters, who looked hard too. He knocked on the unknown man's door. He was much taller than Mr Brown, who had a big belly. He wore the same white vest every day. He was proud of his mound and the stained shirt that covered it.

'Did you do this to my son's football?'

'They were kicking it at my wall.'

'I don't care if they were kicking it at your wall. This is their street. They have lived here their whole lives. You are a blow-in and you have no right to touch their football.'

'I bought this house. This is my wall, paid for with hard-earned cash.'

'Are you saying I don't pay for my flat?'

'I'm saying they were kicking the ball at my wall.'

He went to close his door and Mr Brown put his foot in the way.

'I think we should sort this out now, step outside.'

'You want to fight?'

Mr Brown threw a punch instead of answering. The two of them ended up in the hallway of the house before the fight spilled out on to the road. An unknown woman came out, screaming, with her baby in her arms, as the two men traded blows. She tried to break it up, but was told in no uncertain terms to stay out of it by one of Git's sisters. She ran back inside the house and came out with an empty milk bottle. She smashed it against the front wall of her house. The two men were struggling on the ground when Git ran over and started booting the unknown man in the face. His wife screamed hysterically until they left her husband alone. He went back into the house, bruised and bloodied. Mr Brown walked off, a proud man. The unknown man didn't call the police, but his house was boarded up the next day. A 'For Sale' sign went up the following week. Nobody would buy a boarded-up house, thought Bobby. The Browns pulled the sign down and made the unknown house their own. They would use the window as a door, pulling back the corrugated iron to get in. Mr Brown's actions had given his sons a house for free, albeit one that was boarded up and had no furniture or electricity in it.

'Will I call for you in the morning?' asked Jay.

Bobby knew he couldn't get out of going on the trip to Cork.

'I'll call for you at six. Don't sleep it out.'

Bobby laughed inside at the thought that he might still be asleep at six in the morning. He normally wet the bed at about four and never really went back to sleep properly. It was impossible.

Bobby slept on the bus to Cork. He could sleep

for hours during the day and never wet himself. It was only a nighttime thing.

'I don't want any messing going on in this hotel. You have your keys. We are having dinner here in an hour. It's boring pasta, but it will prepare you for your fights tonight.'

'I don't like pasta,' joked Jay.

'Then you are going to starve and lose your fight.'

Bobby and Jay were in room 213. Bobby didn't think there was enough space for that many bedrooms. He prayed the beds would be far enough apart so he wouldn't disturb Jay in the middle of the night when he had to get up. Jay pushed open the door to the room. They stood staring at the huge double bed.

'Just one bed? I'm not sharing with you,' said Jay as he jumped up onto the bed and grabbed a pillow.

He threw one to Bobby and they whacked each other till their arms were hanging off.

'I'll be too tired to box tonight. Stop.'

'Are you chicken?' asked Jay.

'I'm bollixed. You win.'

Bobby weighed in at thirty-one kilos. The weight limits jumped every three kilos. Jay was going to fight in the thirty-four-kilo weight category. You had to be weighed before the fight and if you weren't the correct weight, you weren't allowed to fight. The club in Cork had clean dressing-rooms and hot showers. It had mirrors on every wall. Bobby couldn't understand a thing the Cork boys were saying.

'Why do they speak like that, Jay?'

'I don't know. Land a punch in their mouths and it will shut them up.'

Bobby was more nervous about sleeping in the same bed as Jay than he was about the fight. He did everything Anto told him. Kept his composure, kept using his jab. He knew he would win after the first thirty seconds. He was able to avoid the punches thrown at him with ease. He landed some brilliant punches that had all the Ballybough boys cheering.

Anto wanted you to fight a particular way. If you went off the script, he went mad. He knew what it took to win fights. Jay decided not to listen to Anto. He came out of his corner all guns blazing. Everyone in the hall could hear the bollocking Anto gave him after the first round. Jay listened and won the next two rounds without trying to knock his opponent out with one punch. He avoided the punches thrown at him, and landed most of the ones he threw.

Anto was proud of all the boxers. He hated losing more than anything. All but one of the Dublin boxers won, but what Anto focused on was Jay's behaviour. He talked about listening and discipline. Bobby knew what he meant. All successful sportsmen were disciplined. Bobby knew he had what it took to become a champion.

'Bobby, are you ever going to go to sleep?'

'I'm not tired.'

'It's half two in the morning. And you're watching shite on the telly.'

Bobby had come up with a simple tactic. Stay awake all night. His eyes grew heavier and heavier. He knew he wouldn't be able to resist the urge. He felt himself drifting off to the place that caused him more pain than anything else in the world. Bobby never woke when he started peeing, only when the last drop came out did he feel himself lying in a puddle. Even though the bed was bigger than anything he had ever slept in, Bobby could still feel Jay's presence beside him. He hung on to the side of the bed, hoping if he did pee, that it would be as far away from Jay as possible.

As usual, Bobby woke on his back, with the puddle beneath him. The clock beside him said it was twenty past four in the morning. He took his pyjamas off and hid them in his bag.

He snuck into the bathroom and took one of the big bath-towels down from its peg. He wrapped it around himself and took the other one down. He folded it in four and tried to place it gently over the wet patch. He looked at Jay's eyes, which were closed. The towel covered the offending area. Bobby lay back down on top of it and pulled the duvet over him. Jay didn't budge. In the thousands of times Bobby had wet the bed, he had never done it twice in one night. The thickness of the towels stopped any of the liquid penetrating through. Bobby stayed awake, dreaming of the day God would give him the ability to stay dry.

One thing Bobby knew was that Jay wasn't thick. He didn't know, or care, what certain words meant, but that didn't make you thick. Pee smelled. And Jay could smell it. Jay looked at the towels. All Bobby could picture was Jay calling him a piss-in-the-bed.

Jay pulled the towel back and stared at the yellow patch. He turned to Bobby and smiled.

'I won't tell Angela.'

'Piss off, I don't fancy her.'

'I pissed in the bed for a while when I was younger.'

'How did you stop?'

'I just grew out of it.'

'My ma says I will too.'

'Of course you will, when you grow up! Don't worry about it, hurry up and get in the shower.'

Bobby showered for as long as Jay would let him.

'There'll be no hot water left.'

'It's a hotel, they have unlimited hot water.'

Bobby loved the feeling of a hot shower on his skin. If he had a shower in his house, it would make his life so much easier.

They sat on top of Ballybough Bridge facing Croke Park, with their trophies and cans beside them. There was a set of traffic lights on the brow of the hill. When they saw the 23 bus coming, Bobby pressed the button. The lights turned orange and then red. As soon as the bus came to a stop, they pulled down their trousers and showed their back-sides to whoever was on the bus.

Willo was crossing at the lights. He reached inside his jacket and pulled out a hammer. He raised it in the air and smashed the passenger window of a Ford Cortina that had stopped at the lights. The lady driver started screaming. Willo grabbed her handbag from the seat. He ran at Bobby and Jay and threw the bag down onto the railway tracks. Willo sprinted off into the flats. Bobby and Jay looked down to see Git running off with the bag. The driver of the bus got off to console the woman.

'What the hell was he doing?' asked Bobby.

'He's a junkie.'

'A what?'

'A druggie. That's why Anto said to stay away from them.'

Jay placed the ball in the middle of the road, directly in front of the boarded-up window of the unknown house.

'A pound says you can't hit it.'

'You're on.'

Jay took aim and just missed the metal window.

'My turn.'

Bobby took aim and hit it direct. Willo stuck his head out.

'What the fuck are you doing?'

'Having a bet to see if we could hit the window,' answered Bobby.

'Give me a shot at that.'

Willo climbed out and Jay placed the ball for him in the middle of the road. Willo lined up to kick it. He pulled his leg back and just as he was about to kick it, Jay pushed the ball out of the way. Willo fell flat on his bum. Bobby and Jay started laughing. Angela was part of a small crowd who were looking on. Willo ran at her and screamed in her face.

'What are you laughing at, nigger?'

'Shut the fuck up,' said Bobby.

'Are you a nigger lover?' Willo hit back.

'Shut up you fucking junkie,' said Bobby.

'What did you say?'

'You're a druggie.'

'Leg it,' shouted Jay.

The two of them sprinted off towards Anto's house. Angela ran off crying. Willo climbed back into the unknown house.

'I have someone I need you to drop off a video to later. I need to show you where it is first.'

Anto walked with them to Sean MacDermott Street, past the swimming pool to a block of flats behind the church. More of the flats were boarded up than occupied.

'Are you sure he has a video recorder? These flats are in bits,' asked Bobby.

'Of course he does.'

They walked into the first block, up the stairwell, which was much darker than Ballybough. The church blocked any light getting in. The flat was right at the end of one of the landings. The door was brown. Anto knocked on the door five times, then a gap, then four times.

'Anto, how are we doing, son?'

Bobby knew Anto wasn't his son. Some inner-city people called everyone son, and didn't know their singular from their plural. Bobby's mam would correct him if he spoke like that.

'Micka, these are my video delivery boys. Bobby and Jay.'

'How are we doing, my sons?'

Maybe he did know his plurals.

'I'll send them down in a while, and I'll see you later.'

'Nice one Anto, son, nice one. Tell them to do the five and four.'

Bobby thought Micka looked like a bit of a mad thing. And so did Johnny for that matter.

'Lads, this is my most precious video. It's Joe Louis, the Brown Bomber, fighting James Braddock for the heavyweight title in 1937.'

'They didn't have televisions in 1937,' joked Jay.

'Now they can put all the old fights on video. Drop this down to Micka.'

When they got there, three people were blocking the entrance to the stairwell. They all had jackets on, even though it was a warm summer day. One of them was Gringo. Bobby got a knot of fear in his stomach. They hadn't seen him since Anto had nearly thrown him off the balcony.

'All right, lads, what are you doing down here?'

'Doing something for Anto,' said Jay, knowing the mention of Anto's name gave them protection.

Jay remembered the knock and banged as hard as he could.

'We have the video for you.'

'What is it?'

'It's Anto's most precious video. The Brown Bomber, Joe Louis,' said Bobby.

'I love the Brown Bomber. Come in for a minute.'

The flat was much nicer than Johnny's. There was a really big television, with videos in front of it on the floor. It was clean. And it had more than one couch. Micka took a tenner off the table and handed it to Jay. He handed a video to Bobby. It had no cover on it.

'Bring this back to Anto and tell him it was perfect.'

Bobby loved running with Jay and Anto, but when he ran on his own he could dream without any distractions. He used each section of his lap to dream about Angela. His record time for the 2,300-metre lap was just under nine minutes. He had a digital watch, which he used to time himself. Eight minutes, fifty-six seconds, and seventy-seven hundredths of a second. 8:56.77. He scraped it on the headboard of his bed. He had the number imprinted on his brain but he always dreamed about running faster.

To the top of the bridge into Summerhill Parade was five hundred metres. He would dream about holding Angela's hand walking up Ballybough Road. It was harder to run uphill at the start, but athletics were run in a clockwise direction, so Bobby's lap had to be, too. He could have started at the Sunset House, but that meant finishing there, and it was farther away from his house. It also meant running along in front of the flats for the last bit of the lap. He liked running that bit at the start when he had more energy, just in case he saw someone he knew. When he got to the Sunset, he looked at the watch; he knew he wanted it to be just under three minutes. It was just under a third of the way. He looked at the watch, 2:40.

Brilliant, thought Bobby. Get to the corner of Jones's Road in just under two minutes. He would focus on Angela kissing him at the Sunset, and pick up the pace slightly, accelerating again when he turned the corner at Hogan's pub. He looked at the watch, four minutes exactly.

Bobby took a few deep breaths and tried to work out how fast he could run the five-hundred-metre stretch behind the Hogan Stand. It was fifty metres longer than the last bit, but it had a long downhill stretch. Angela would let him touch her breasts on the outside of her top. He got to the top of the bridge and accelerated down. He focused on the gates of Holy Cross College.

When he turned onto Clonliffe Road he looked at the watch again, 5:32. He worked out that he had to run the final six hundred and fifty metres in 3:24 to beat his record. His legs were beginning to feel like they weighed ten stone each. It was time to think of touching Angela breasts on the inside of her top, but instead he imagined he was Eamonn

Coghlan catching the Russian athlete in Helsinki at the World Championships in 1983. Coghlan was so confident he was going to win that he glanced at the Russian athlete and smiled. He was Ireland's first ever athletics world champion. Dig deep for one final effort. He counted the sixteen single-storey redbrick houses as he passed them. He was halfway along the final stretch.

His lungs were burning but it didn't slow him down, he just focused on being Eamonn Coghlan. When he got to the end, he stopped the watch. 8:30.01. Twenty-six seconds faster. It gave him a sick feeling in his stomach, but it made his brain feel good.

CHAPTER 7

Bobby's mam watched every news programme on the television. Even if the headlines were the same on the six o'clock news and the nine o'clock news, she still watched them both. It wouldn't be on the news unless it was bad news. Watching it never made you happy. It was always about explosions in Northern Ireland or England. Bobby couldn't understand why she wanted to watch bad news.

The noise the door getting kicked in made was like an explosion. It wasn't the first time that the house had been targeted. But now Bobby knew it was his fault. He ran out onto the stairs and saw the hall door lying on the floor. It had come clean off the hinges. It had been happening for years. Normally in the dark of winter, the older lads in the flats would throw stones at the windows. At Halloween they would throw fireworks in the letterbox. It upset Bobby's mam more than anything. She wanted to leave the area. People had come to view the house and were interested in buying, but Bobby's mam felt guilty that they would have fireworks put in their letterbox. She couldn't bear to pass on that situation so she decided to live with it, as hard as it was.

'Will you run and get your dad?'

Bobby had to step on the door to get out. He knew she was sad that his dad loved the pub more than the house. Bobby had heard the words 'one for the road' so many times he had lost count. He still loved going to the Sunset to get him though. Bobby felt bad; he knew it was Willo who had kicked the door in. It was his fault for calling him a junkie.

It only took him two minutes to get to the Sunset if he sprinted down the main road. He decided to take his alternative route. He pretended he was escaping from the Black and Tans.

Down Ardilaun Road, up the railings at the end, onto the railway tracks. Up onto the grass bank that ran between the railway tracks and the canal. Up the wall that led to the top of Ballybough Bridge.

The stones that made up the wall of the bridge were large grey blocks. There was a gap big enough between the blocks for Bobby to put his size-three runners into. He could haul himself up bit by bit until he reached the top. It was a long way down. About fifteen feet. Bobby had counted the blocks. There were eighteen from top to bottom. They were each nine inches high. Eighteen times nine is a hundred and sixty-two. He also knew there were twelve inches in a foot. His ruler for school was twelve inches long. Or thirty centimetres. One hundred and sixty two divided by twelve was about thirteen. There was also cement in between each block. Bobby reckoned that made it fifteen feet high.

'Dad, mam wants you,' Bobby said, panting, having just escaped from the Black and Tans.

'Do you want a Coke?'

'Mam said she needs you.'

'John, get the young fella a Coke, please.'

The barman in the Sunset had been there for as long as the pub. He moved really slowly due to his old age, and walked with his back hunched forwards. Bobby poured the tiny bottle of Coke into his glass of ice, deciding the news could wait a few minutes. The cold Coke going down his throat was the nicest taste in the world. He took a small sup at a time, to get as much value out of the small bottle as he could.

'John, I'll have one for the road.'

'A pint, Matt?'

'And a short, thanks.'

'Dad, the door was kicked in. It was knocked off the hinges.'

Matt was brilliant at fixing things. He had the door hanging back up in no time. Laura didn't even have to ask him not to go back to the pub. Bobby could hear his mother's concerns.

'We can't raise children in this area.'

Matt listened intently to what she was saying. Bobby was afraid his dad was coming to the same conclusion as his mam.

'We'll put the house up for sale again.'

'But nobody will buy it.'

'We might get lucky.'

He had to tell Jay as quickly as possible. The last time there was talk of moving out was when fireworks had been put through the letterbox three nights in a row.

'My mam wants to move out now and it's my fault.'

'How is it your fault?' asked Jay.

'Cause I called Willo a junkie.'

'He *is* a junkie.'

'I should have said nothing.'

'Did you tell Anto?' Jay wanted to know.

'Why would I tell him?'

'He always says if we have a problem to talk to him.'

Anto was livid that Bobby's door had been touched. Bobby had never told him about the fireworks and the rocks. Jay told him exactly what was going on now, the fear of losing his friend sparking him into action.

'I'm sorry about this, Mrs Ryan. I'm going to have a word with who I think is responsible.'

'I don't want to be bringing more trouble on us.'

'It will be the end of your trouble.'

'I'd appreciate that, Anto.'

Anto made them stand outside while he went into the unknown house. Bobby was worried that Anto might make the situation worse. They could hear shouting and then quiet. Anto came out the window first, followed by Git and then Willo.

'There is going to be an apology. If you can't manage that then we can sort it out another way.'

Anto marched them down the road and knocked gently on the door.

'They have something to say, Mrs Ryan.'

'It was me who kicked the door and I'm sorry,' said Willo, while he looked at the ground.

'And you?'

'Sorry, Mrs Ryan.'

Git looked like the whole idea was Willo's. He would always go along with anything his brother did. Bobby couldn't believe what he had just seen. Normally, violence was used to sort out problems in the inner city. His dad had been threatening for ages to kick the lads' heads in, if he could catch them. Anto had sorted it out with words. The hassle had gone on for years and Matt had been able do nothing about it. Bobby knew it was because Anto was from the flats. He wanted them to live in the flats. If they lived in a flat, nobody would see them as different. Why couldn't they just move to the flats? He hated being different.

Thirteen was a lucky number for Bobby. He was born on 13 July, and he could sneeze thirteen times in a row. He had also seen thirteen magpies on a telegraph wire one day. He won a bet on a horse call Thurles Connection that day. It was number thirteen. He didn't believe thirteen was unlucky.

His dad had asked him what he wanted for his birthday and there could only be one answer. He described the shirt in detail, explaining exactly where it was in the shop. Tony Ward's sports shop in town had a bargain bin of old jerseys and a rack of all the latest football shirts. On the new rack was the brand new Liverpool shirt, sponsored by Crown Paints. It was written in yellow across the front of the red shirt. Bobby loved the way it looked. It was fourteen pounds ninety-nine pence.

It was always the same deal. Into his parents' room to open his card first. It always had a footballer on the front. The message said, 'Happy 13th Birthday, enjoy the jersey. I hope it makes you play better. Love, mam and dad. XXX.' He ripped open the present and saw white. It was a white jersey. He looked at the front of it, and it was the old England jersey they had worn in the 1982 World

Cup. It had an Admiral logo on the front and a blue and red stripe. He loved England, they were much better than Ireland, but Liverpool were the best.

'What do you think?'

'Thanks Dad,' was all he could muster, knowing it was from the bargain bin in Tony Ward's.

A fiver was all he was worth. He begrudgingly gave them both a kiss and went to walk out of the room.

'Try it on.'

'I need to have a wash first.'

He came upstairs after his washing ritual with the jersey on. He looked at himself in the mirror but all he wanted to see was the Liverpool shirt.

'It looks great, thanks a million,' he lied.

'I thought you would love it. I know you love Kevin Keegan.'

'Happy birthday, English boy,' laughed Jay.

'Piss off, it's a Kevin Keegan shirt.'

'An England Kevin Keegan shirt.'

'I asked for the new Liverpool shirt and this is what I got.'

'Are you coming into town?'

'I'm not robbing any jeans.'

'Do you fancy a few games of Mario Brothers? I'll put five credits into it for your birthday.'

'Thanks a million.'

Bobby couldn't get the Liverpool shirt out of his

head. After a few hours playing Mario, he had a plan.

'Let's go after this game.'

'Where to?'

'To the bookies. I'm going to win the money to buy the shirt.'

'You're mad. What if you lose the money?'

'I had nothing to begin with, so if I end up with nothing then I'm just back where I started.'

'You say that every time. You have to have something to start with if you are going to put the bet on.'

Every bookie in Dublin was next door to a pub. It provided another way for the alcoholics to lose their money, or to win some for more drink. Or to win some for a new football shirt. Bobby could read the form of horses. Sometimes horses were in good form, sometimes bad. The same as humans. The key to winning a bet was to predict what form they would be in. A row of numbers beside their name signified where they had finished in their last few races. A zero meant it had finished nowhere. A one meant it had won the last race it ran. The number two beside the name meant it finished second. It was important to be able to read the form. The *Sporting Life* listed the finishing time of each horse and the distance of each race it ran. The summer was the flat-racing season. The horses went over jumps in the winter, when the ground was softer, so that the jockeys wouldn't completely wreck themselves when they fell off going thirty miles an hour. The shortest races were five furlongs. A furlong was two hundred metres. Eight furlongs was a mile.

Ladbrokes on O'Connell Street was just around the corner from Barney's video arcade. It was Bobby's favourite bookies because they had free coffee and tea. It was illegal to gamble if you were under eighteen, but Bobby had never been stopped. He had been questioned a few times but he just said the bet was for his dad. Bobby grabbed some dockets and a bookie's pencil. He looked up at the board that listed all the races. The 2.15 at Catterick was ten minutes away from starting. There were ten runners. It was a seven-furlong sprint. Number 13 was called Jack the Lad.

'That has to be a sign. Thirteen is my lucky number and it's a seven-furlong sprint.'

'You're as mad as your da. What does it matter if it's a seventy-furlong sprint?'

'A seventy-furlong sprint isn't a sprint because seventy furlongs is over eight miles.'

'Just put the bet on.'

Bobby checked the *Sporting Life*. Beside the horse's name it said, 'Course and distance winner'.

This rang a bell for Bobby. His dad had about ten thousand superstitions when it came to gambling.

Never back a favourite in a three-horse race.

He had heard that so many times and thought it was the most ridiculous one. Another one was *course and distance winner.* Some days it was a reason to back a horse, other days it was the reason a horse would lose. Half of his superstitions contradicted the other half.

Jack the Lad was 4–1. Pat Eddery was in the saddle. Bobby knew if he put three pounds on it would give him fifteen back.

'I'm going to put three quid on Jack the Lad.'

Bobby climbed up on one of the stools to write the bet out.

£3 win Jack the Lad, 2.15 Catterick.

The lady behind the counter was looking at him suspiciously.

'Is it OK if I do a bet for my dad? He is in the pub next door.'

'Of course it is, son, do you know which horse he wants to back?'

At that moment, Bobby remembered another one of his dad's superstitions.

'Never write out a bet with a bookie's pencil.'

He didn't listen to that voice in his head the last time and he lost.

'No I'll go and ask him, thanks.'

'Come on, Jay, quick, we need to find a shop.'

'For what?'

'We need to buy a pen and we need to pretend we're asking my dad which horse he wants to back.'

'You just wrote out the bet.'

'I know, it was with a bookie's pencil, though.'

'It doesn't make any difference, you lunatic.'

There was a shop a few doors down from the bookies.

'Can I have a pen please?'

'What type of pen, we have Bic biros, felt tips…'

'What is the cheapest?'

'The Bic, it's five pence. We have them in blue, black, red…'

'Any colour will do, red actually.'

Liverpool wore red. Bobby had three pound twenty left. He knew a three-pound bet would cost three pound thirty with the ten per cent tax added on.

'Can I borrow ten pence off you, Jay?'

'No.'

'What do you mean, no?'

'Not for a bet. I'm not giving you money for a bet.'

'Pretend it's for a Mint Crisp then.'

Jay begrudgingly handed over the ten pence. Bobby took out a fresh docket. He started writing out the bet. He always heard voices in his head when he was writing out a bet.

Do the bet. Back another horse. Put the money back in your pocket.

'*Last few loading at Catterick,*' came across the tannoy.

He wrote the bet out again.

£3 win Jack the Lad 2.15 Catterick.

'That's three thirty please.'

He made the Sign of the Cross in the palm of his hand with his index finger. He could feel his heart racing.

'*Jack the Lad has drifted in the market betting. They're off at Catterick at 2.16.*'

Bobby walked back to Jay.

'If the horse wins, don't get excited or they might think we put the bet on for ourselves.'

'OK, why has it drifted?'

'It's not fancied on the track, so the odds drift. It doesn't make a difference really, just means I win more money.'

They both stared intently at the small television in the corner of the bookies. Two old men were dragging on their smokes, directly under the TV. They had to stand close to see the screen. One of them shouted, 'Go on number two.'

Some old men backed numbers without even looking at the form. Bobby looked up at the board. Number two. Red Mist. 33–1. The commentary for the race was crackly.

Red Mist leads by about four lengths. Two furlongs

to go. The pack are chasing him down. Red Mist still holding on by four lengths.

Bobby felt a knot grow in his stomach, as his heart started to beat a bit faster. He should have backed Red Mist. It was a red jersey he was looking for, a red pen he wrote the bet with, and Red Mist was 33–1. He had three pounds. That would have been ninety-nine pounds winnings. He started to feel sick.

A furlong to go. Red Mist still leads. Clockwork Orange is closing, so is Jack the Lad. Pat Eddery is closing with every stride on Jack the Lad.

Eddery was his dad's favourite jockey, when he won him a bet. He was a bastard, bollix and any other insulting term he could think of when he lost a race.

One hundred yards to go. They're neck and neck. Fifty yards to go. It's too close to call. A photo finish between Jack the Lad, Red Mist and Clockwork Orange.

'Do you think you won?'

'I think Jack the Lad got up on the line. It's hard to tell. Eddery is a genius, as my da would say.'

This one is gone to the judges. Very close. Its looks to me as if the outsider, Red Mist, has pulled off a surprise, with Willie Carson on board.

The old smoker under the television got a big hug from his friend.

'Willie Carson is a genius. We'll have a few pints on him tonight.'

They both lit up another cigarette and looked like the most contented couple in the world.

Result in from Catterick. First, number two, Red Mist. Second, number seven, Jack the Lad. Third, number four, Clockwork Orange. The SPs. 33–1, 9–2 and 7–4 favourite.

The SP stood for Starting Price. Bobby thought it should have been FP, for finishing price. He felt sicker than he had ever felt doing a bet. He normally put fifty pence on. That was his limit. If he lost, he left the bookies. If he won, he put another fifty pence on. He always limited his losses. Bobby scrunched up the docket and threw it on the floor. Jay pretended he was the commentator on the race.

'First, number two, Red Mist, second number seven...'

'Piss off.'

They walked out of the bookies in silence.

'I'm going down to my mam to get a red apple.'

'Ha, ha.'

'Or a lovely orange.'

'I'm going home.'

His heart was racing, and he still had the sick feeling in his stomach. He could hear voices in his head telling him he should have done this or he should have done that. Why didn't he back Red Mist? He would have over a hundred pounds in his pocket if he had. When he got home, he sat on his bed staring at Croke Park, swearing he would never gamble again, but deep down he knew he would. The sick feeling always left him eventually, leaving him free to have another bet.

Bobby could wallow in the mire for hours. He only knew what that meant because his brother had a Doors LP. Eventually, Jay knocked.

'What have you been doing?'

'Wallowing.'

'What?'

'Being pissed off.'

'I got you a present.'

Jay had never got him a present before.

'It's a free bet with Ladbrokes.'

'It doesn't look like a free bet.'

The present was small and long and was wrapped in masking tape.

'If you can't guess what it is, then you can't have it.'

'It looks like a load of masking tape wrapped around a cucumber.'

'You got it in one. Here.'

Bobby started to unwrap the masking tape. It was tied so tight that it took ages. Underneath it was plastic. When he had enough of the tape off, he ripped the plastic open to reveal something red.

'It's a Red Mist.'

'It's the Liverpool shirt,' screamed Bobby.

'Happy birthday.'

'Thanks, Jay.'

Bobby pulled off the England shirt and put the Liverpool one on.

'Did you look at the back?'

Bobby had to take it off again to look at the back. It had the number seven on it.

'How did you get a number on it?'

'Tony Ward can put them on. Number seven, Red Mist.'

'Red Mist was number two and I'm never betting again.'

'Yeah, right.'

'Never three quid anyway.' '

Bobby couldn't believe Jay had spent fifteen pounds on a jersey for him. He wanted to wear it in bed but didn't want to wet it. So he hung it from the laths of the top bunk, and stared at it for ages. First the front, then the number seven. It would remain his most treasured possession.

CHAPTER 8

Anto handed them another video cassette and sent them on their way. At the top of Sackville Avenue, Jay turned to Bobby.

'How can Anto make money renting videos?'

'It doesn't cost him anything to make them.'

'But how much does he pay us to deliver them? It's a tenner for this one, right?'

'Yeah.'

'And is Micka paying a tenner for this video?'

'Maybe he's just doing it because he's their friend.'

'Does Anto look like he would be friends with them?'

'What are you saying?'

'How much is it to rent a video?'

'It's one pound for the new releases in Xtra-vision.'

'Exactly.'

'So what are you saying?'

'Let's go up to my flat.'

'For what?'

'I want to check something.'

'What are you checking?'
'Just wait and see.'

When they got there, Jay took the video out of the box. He examined it, pressing the button on the side to lift up the part that protected the tape.
'What are you doing?'
'I think there's something in here.'
'What are you on about?'
Jay shook the video and it made a rattling noise.
'See?'
'Don't be stupid, all videos make a rattling noise when you shake them.''
Jay got a small screwdriver. On the back of the video cassette, there were three screws. He unscrewed them and lifted the back off. Inside were three packages wrapped in clingfilm. Jay unwrapped one of the small packages. Inside, was a white powdery substance. He poked at it with the screwdriver.
'I don't think we should be doing this, Jay.'
'Do you know what it is?'
'I think so.'
He poked at it again.
'What are you doing?'
'I'm going to snort it.'
'What?'
Jay put his nose up to the package.

'I'm only messing. How much is it worth? What do you reckon?'

'I haven't got a clue.'

'If one of them is worth a hundred quid, then how much is all that worth?'

'Three hundred quid, you dope.'

'It's worth a lot more than that.'

'Put them back in and let's go.'

Bobby had a really big knot in his stomach walking into Summerhill Parade. He knew they shouldn't be bringing the video to Micka.

'Why is Anto sending us up with this?'

'He trusts us.'

'Jay, it's heroin. It's not right. We could get in trouble. My mam will kill me if she finds out.'

'How will she find out?'

'I don't know. I'm nervous.'

'It's just a video.'

'It's not just a video.'

'You have to think it is. Just like the jeans. If I walk out of the shop thinking I'm going to be caught, I will be caught. I'll look guilty if I start panicking.'

'I'm starting to panic.'

'Turn around and go home then.'

They stopped on top of the bridge. Bobby leaned on the wall looking into the canal below.

'I'll knock for you in the morning. We can go and spend my tenner.'

'You can keep the tenner, I'm coming with you,' said Bobby.

'No panic allowed.'

'None.'

Bobby knew he couldn't turn back. He had been fighting for acceptance from Jay for years. Bobby knew he was a chicken sometimes. Jay was never a chicken. Whether it was robbing jeans or orchards or orange juice, Jay never showed any fear. He believed he could do anything. Bobby wanted to be like Jay and have no fear. He didn't want to be seen as different, and he certainly didn't want to be considered a chicken. If Jay had decided to turn back, Bobby would have turned back with him.

'Will we jog down? That will take your mind off it.'

Jogging didn't keep either of their minds off it. They dropped the video off and looked at the fellas hanging around the flats in a different way.

'I'm not delivering any more videos,' Bobby announced just before they were about to get in the ring.

'OK.'

'Are you serious?'

'Yeah. One more and then we'll stop.'

'Why one more?'

'Have we got a deal?'

'Come on lads, you're delaying everyone,' Anto shouted at them.

'Have we got a deal, Bobby?'

'Right, one more. If you promise to stop.'

'Are you chatting or boxing?'

'Chatting and boxing, Anto. Muhammad Ali could do it.'

'You're far from Muhammad Ali, Jay. Quit the chatting. Three one-minute rounds.'

They boxed as hard as they could for the three minutes. You didn't have time to think about anything when somebody was throwing punches. The feeling of a punch flush on the nose hurt, but made Bobby smile at same time. He had learned how to keep his composure when hit. Anto always told them to pretend like it didn't hurt. 'Smile back at your opponent,' he would say. 'You have to have a poker face.' Jay couldn't do that. When Bobby caught him with a flush punch, he would go mad throwing as many punches as he could with no co-ordination whatsoever. Bobby could easily duck out of the way. They both loved bloody noses. They were the sign of a successful night in the ring.

'I'll see youse tomorrow. Call over at lunch time,' Anto told them quietly as they left the club.

Jay was giddy and had the usual bounce in his step. Bobby walked much slower, Jay telling him to 'hurry up' every time he fell a few steps behind.

'Are we going to tell him we are just stopping?'

'You'll see,' said Jay, frustrating Bobby by withholding information.

'What are we going to do?'

'I have a plan.'

'What is it?'

'Do you promise to go along with what I say?'

'How can I promise if I don't know what you're going to say?'

'What if we get robbed on our way to do a delivery?'

'What?' Bobby interrupted.

'Listen, will you? If the video gets robbed before we deliver it, then Anto will stop us delivering them. We won't have to say anything.'

'That's your master plan?'

'Yeah. It's perfect.'

'It's stupid.'

'What do you suggest, Bobby the brainbox?'

'We just tell him we're stopping.'

'OK. Anto, we're not delivering the videos any more because we know what's in them. Is that what you're going to say?'

Bobby knew Jay had a point, but he didn't think his plan would work.

'Bobby, I want to stop too. But we can't say it to him or he'll know we opened it.'

'Right,' said Bobby stubbornly.

'I'll come up with a story about being robbed.

If we both stick to it we'll be fine.'

Bobby lay in bed for hours worrying about everything. When he couldn't sleep, he would say an Our Father, followed by a Hail Mary, repeatedly until he began to get tired. When he started forgetting the words of the prayers, he knew he was nearly there.

Jay answered the door like he hadn't a worry in the world.

'Good morning, good morning.'

'What has you so happy?'

'I have the story.'

'Go on then.'

'We'll say that when we got to the bottom of Micka's stairwell, there were three lads standing there. All of them had hoods pulled up on their heads. Two of them grabbed us by the arms and the third one grabbed the video. Simple.'

'Simple. What if we have to go to Johnny's?'

'We'll just say Johnny's stairwell then.'

Anto gave them the video, unaware of what was about to happen. Jay rightly predicted it was Micka who would be receiving it. They left the video in Jay's bedroom and jogged down to Micka's. They took off at a slow pace, without talking. By the time they passed the Red Brick Slaughterhouse on Rutland Street, Bobby could see his chest expanding, he was breathing so heavily.

He wasn't jogging very fast, yet he was out of breath. They stopped jogging at the swimming pool and walked across the courtyard of the church. There was nobody at the bottom of the stairwell.

'You stay quiet and let me do the talking.'

Jay kicked on Micka's door as loud as he could. Four boots, followed by five.

'Your video was robbed.'

'What?'

'Someone grabbed us and robbed your video.'

'Who?'

'I don't know. Goodbye.'

'Goodbye nothing. What did they look like?'

'I don't know. At the top of the stairs, three people grabbed us and ran off with the video.'

'What did they look like?' Micka growled at the lads.

'They all had hoods up, we couldn't see them,' said Jay.

Micka sprinted down the stairs. They could see him from the balcony running around looking for someone that didn't exist. It was a long walk back to Anto's. Bobby couldn't believe what was happening, but he knew they had to stop delivering the videos.

'What are we going to say to Anto?'

'Exactly what we just said to Micka.'

'You told him it happened at the top of the stairs.'

'I said the bottom.'

'You said the top, so say the same to Anto.'

'Are you sure?'

Bobby gave him the look without answering. Jay knew when Bobby was being serious.

They walked slowly back to Ballybough. Jay was excited. He wouldn't stop talking about the look on Micka's face.

'We need to do something else.'

'Another master plan?'

'No, you need to punch me on the nose. Make it bleed.'

Jay closed his eyes.

'Hit me.'

'No, hit yourself.'

Jay tried to punch himself on the nose but he was unable to do it with enough force. It was much easier to hit someone else.

'I need you to do it. I'll close my eyes and count to three.'

Jay closed his eyes again.

'One.'

He opened them to see what Bobby was doing.

'Close your eyes.'

'One, two.'

Bobby didn't wait for three. He landed a stiff punch flush on Jay's nose.

'Aaaaargh. Jesus, that hurt.'

'It was supposed to.'

Jay put his finger up his left nostril to feel for the blood. He took the finger out and there was no sign of blood on it. A trickle began to leave his right nostril. Jay smiled as it reached his lip.

'We have blood. Let's go,' he announced.

'Are you going to do the talking?'

'Leave it to me.'

Anto answered the door with no top on. He had a six-pack stomach. Bobby had done thousands of sit-ups, like Anto had told him, and he didn't have any muscles.

'What happened?'

He could see the blood because Jay had spread it to make it look more dramatic.

'Did Micka get the video?'

'No.'

'What do you mean?'

'Three fellas grabbed us and took the video.'

'Who were they? What did they look like?'

'They had their hoods up, we couldn't see them.'

'You must have seen something, Bobby.'

'It all happened so quick. Jay wouldn't let it go. He tried to stop them. And one of them punched him.'

'Where did this happen?'

'On the stairwell of Micka's flat,' explained Jay, 'I tried to stop them.'

Jay pretended to get upset.

'Don't worry. Don't worry.'

'Why would a junkie rob a boxing video?' asked Jay.

'How do you know they were junkies?'

'All the fellas down there look like junkies.'

Anto ran back inside and put a top on, before sprinting past them down the road.

'I wouldn't let it go.'

'I thought it sounded realistic.'

'It did. You're good.'

Bobby got a little bit of a buzz being believed by Anto. He didn't suspect a thing.

'Now what are we going to do with the video?'

Bobby wanted to know the next part of Jay's master plan.

'What do you want to do with it?'

'I think we should throw it in the canal.'

The only things they had ever thrown into the canal were rocks, at the dirty rats that lived under the bridges.

'We should see what's in it first.'

'We're not opening it.'

'We can't throw all that money in the canal.'

'It's not money.'

'Are you not curious about how much it's worth?'

'No. And neither are you. We're getting rid of the video.'

'We can get rid of the video, without the drugs in it.'

Jay started to unscrew the video.

'I'm going home, you're doing it on your own.'

Bobby was only home for ten minutes when Jay knocked.

'Anto wants the two of us. He has his own plan.'

'I'm going to follow behind the two of you. If anyone tries to touch you I will be there to pounce. I want to try and find out who it is. Don't look behind you or act suspiciously,' he informed them.

'Did you find out who robbed us?' enquired Jay.

'They didn't rob you. They just borrowed something that belonged to me and when I find out who it was, they will give it back,' Anto said, with a certainty that they believed.

'What will you do to them?'

'Bobby, that doesn't matter. What matters is respect. They will learn not to disrespect me.'

'But that's twice now that we have been robbed. Those videos are bringing us bad luck,' said Jay.

'It won't happen again. I won't have you going into the flats to meet Micka.'

'What about Johnny?'

'Or Johnny.'

'It's a waste you giving us a fiver every time. Sure they may as well call here to collect the videos,' said Bobby.

'They are lazy swines. Micka will meet you outside the swimming pool. Off you go.'

They walked to the top of the bridge. Bobby couldn't resist and turned around for a look. Anto was halfway up the hill behind them.

'I thought it was the last delivery.'

'So did I.'

The shop beside the Red Brick Slaughterhouse was the dirtiest shop in Dublin. Jay said it smelled like old women. It was in the front room of one of the three-storey houses. Two floors above ground and a basement below. Everyone threw rubbish into the basement.

'Let's go in, Bobby.'

'Anto will go mad.'

'Just don't look behind. It's only a video so we have to act normal. He hasn't a clue what really happened.'

The hall door was always wide open to signify that the shop was open for business. The minute you stepped inside the hallway, a dog, which was behind a gate leading up the stairs, would bark its head off. It had the loudest bark Bobby had ever heard. The shop was in a door off to the right of the hall. Two old women ran the shop. They wore the same dirty aprons every day. The shop smelled like old person mixed with sweets. The selection of sweets wasn't that great, but one thing they always had was flying saucers. They were delicious and only a halfpenny each.

'Ten flying saucers, please,' said Bobby.

'Excuse me?'

The dog was still barking and the deaf old woman couldn't hear. Bobby pointed to the big box of flying saucers and put ten fingers in the air. She had to bring the box below the counter to open it because she was so crouched over from old age. The brown bag came back with the ten pink and yellow flying saucers.

'Twenty flying saucers please,' asked Jay.

'Twenty, I'll have another ten please too.'

'Give me that bag so and I'll put them in it, I'm not wasting bags on the two of you.'

They both put a flying saucer in their mouths. Inside was sherbet powder. The outside stuck to your tongue and the roof of your mouth, but within a few seconds the saliva broke through the shell and released the taste of the sherbet.

Bobby and Jay would have competitions to see who could keep their mouth closed the longest. When they came out they could see Anto leaning against a railing about ten houses up from the shop. He had his arms crossed and looked annoyed. They fell around the corner laughing and into Sean MacDermott Street. They could see Micka waiting at the closed entrance to the swimming pool.

'Sorry about what happened lads, it will never happen again.'

They couldn't respond, as their mouths were full of flying saucer and the first to open it was the loser. Jay tried to respond with his mouth full but all that came out was noise. The two of them laughed even more. Bobby handed over the video. Micka waved at Anto who was at the corner of Rutland Street, thirty yards away. They turned to walk towards Anto, but he had disappeared. When they got to Rutland Street, he was nowhere to be seen.

'Race you,' shouted Jay.

The two of them took off at full pace, flying down Ballybough Road.

'Race you to the bridge.'

Bobby pipped Jay for the victory. It took them half the downhill side of the bridge to slow down.

'I beat you again.'

'Piss off. Put money on it and I'll beat you.'

'The length of Sackville Avenue. A fiver.'

'The fiver is mine, Bobby.'

They took off. Jay had a lead of a couple of yards. They were heading full pace towards the finish line. Bobby was catching Jay gradually, but as they got to the end, Jay won easily. Bobby realised that when Jay wanted to beat him, he always could. Most of the time he didn't try his best, but when he did, he could always beat Bobby.

CHAPTER 9

Anto made them tell their story again and again after boxing. He wrote down every bit of descriptive detail they could think of. Bobby knew it was to see if their story changed at all. Jay was convinced he believed them and was staking out Micka's flat for the day so he could exact his revenge. They had their stories straight. Bobby was surprised how easy it was to lie. He pictured the three of them at the top of the stairs, just like Jay had told him. Red top, black top and blue top. All looked in their twenties. They kept the info as simple as possible.

'I remember one of them had an earring. It was a gold stud.'

'Which one, Jay?'

'The one with the red top.'

'Which ear was it in?'

Jay had to think for a moment. He put his hand up to his own ear. He found it hard to tell his right from his left. He pointed to Anto's right ear.

'It was in that one.'

'Any other information, Bobby?'

He closed his eyes and pictured them again.

'The one with the black top had Gola runners on. Grey ones. I looked down and saw them. My brother has the exact same pair, that's how I remember.'

Jay looked at him, proud of the convincing friend he had. Anto went off with his notes on the suspects.

'Are you going to come with me?' Jay asked Bobby, when they got outside.

'Where?'

'To the unknown house.'

'For what?'

'To find out how much it's worth.'

'No. I'm going home.'

Bobby didn't want Jay thinking he was scared, but he was.

'I'll tell you how much it's worth in the morning.'

He stared out the window of his bedroom, worrying. He couldn't understand why Jay wanted to open the video, and why he was interested in finding out anything about it.

He listened to his mam answer the knock on the front door.

'Bobby. It's Jay.'

He walked slowly down the stairs, pretending not to be too excited that Jay was there.

'I can't go on my own. I need you to come with me.'

'Why do you have to go at all?'

'Are you not curious?'

'Shush. My mam will hear you.'

'Are you coming?'

Bobby went in and told his mam he was going out to kick ball.

'Don't be long.'

'I'll just be outside.'

Jay threw the ball at the window of the unknown house.

'We know it's worth money. Why do we need to find out how much?'

'Bobby, just play it cool.'

Willo pushed the corrugated iron out.

'What do you want?'

'I want to show you something.'

'Show me then.'

'We'll have to come inside.'

Bobby immediately felt his heart begin to race faster than it had ever done before. He could feel a layer of sweat build on his back as his whole body heated up. He felt out of breath.

'Climb in so.'

Willo held the corrugated iron window open for them as they climbed in.

'This place is bleeding filthy,' laughed Jay.

He nudged Bobby and pointed at the ground.

'Do you even know what this is for?' asked Git, as he picked up the needle.

'Yeah I do,' Jay answered back quickly.

He reached into his underpants and pulled out a package. It was a small amount of one the bigger packages. It was wrapped in cling film. He placed it on the ground in front of Willo and Git and opened it.

'You put this in it.'

'Jesus,' Willo said as he looked closely at the powder. 'Where did you get that?'

'That's only flour or something. Are you fucking messing with us?'

'Shut up you,' said Willo. 'This is the real thing. Where did the two of you get this from?'

'I found it in the stairwell,' said Jay.

'Some fucking eejit dropped that in the stairwell,' said Bobby. 'And we want to know how much it is worth.'

Jay looked at him with a sense of disbelief as Bobby asserted himself.

'It's worth nothing because it's mine. I dropped it there. Now piss off.'

'We'll piss off if you tell us how much it's worth,' said Jay, determined not to leave without an answer.

'Fifty quid.'

'Show us what you do with it.'

'Jay, when you do it, you go to heaven,' Willo said.

'Show me.'

Willo picked up a spoon and emptied a small amount of the powder onto it. He then poured some water onto the spoon. He held a lighter under the spoon. The boys moved closer and could see the water starting to bubble. It started to turn a dark brown colour. Willo dropped the inside of a cigarette butt carefully onto the spoon. He put the tip of the needle into the butt and sucked the liquid into the needle. Bobby could feel an eerie quiet, but was transfixed by the whole operation. Git tightened a belt around his brother's arm so his veins bulged. Bobby thought it looked like Marco Tardelli's. Willo pierced the vein with the needle, sucked some blood into in and then pushed the mixture into his arm. He loosened the belt and fell back on the couch.

'Is it good? Is it good?'

Git was anxious to know.

'Is it good? Is it good?'

He couldn't contain his excitement.

'Unfuckingbelieveable.'

Git grabbed the spoon and began to repeat the process. Bobby and Jay looked at each other.

'Let's go,' Jay whispered.

Willo and Git paid no notice to them getting out

the window. Bobby was happy he was out, but glad he had had the bravery to go in.

'If that's worth fifty, then that whole video is worth thousands.'

'Then we have to get rid of it.'

'I think we should sell it.'

'To who?'

'Willo and Git.'

'Are you gone stone cold mad?'

'I'll race you for it.'

'What do you mean "for it"?'

'If I win, we sell it. If you win, we dump it in the canal.'

'This plan of yours was supposed to stop the deliveries. Now we're being followed by Anto and you want to sell some of the stuff. Too right I'll race you for it, and for no more deliveries. The loser has to say to Anto "no more deliveries". Have we got a deal?'

'Jesus, take a breath. We have a deal. Where do you want to race?'

'A lap of Croker.'

When they normally raced a lap of Croker, they would take it easy all the way around and then have a sprint finish down Clonliffe Road. If you went too fast at the start, you burned out before the end.

'How are you feeling?'

Bobby didn't answer him. He was formulating

a race plan in his head. It was the final of the Olympic Games. He would be a national hero if he won. He didn't want to think about the deliveries.

'Are you chicken that I'll beat you again?'

Bobby took a deep breath. He just stared straight ahead.

'Are you going to speak?'

Bobby shook his head. Speaking would be wasted energy.

'Fine.'

Bobby felt in the zone. He wanted go faster than his 8:30 record time. He decided on his race tactics: go quick at the start to try and burn Jay off. He set off down Ballybough Road at a blistering pace. Jay was a few yards behind him. He could hear him breathing heavily.

'You won't be able to keep that pace going.'

Bobby knew he mightn't be able to keep the pace going, but his tactics were to try and get Jay's legs to start burning before his. If he could do that, then Jay might have to slow down or might even give up. When he got to the top of the bridge at the Hogan Stand, he looked behind and saw that Jay had dropped five yards behind. Bobby was pushing it as hard as he could. He decided to give it one last push down the hill past Croke Park. He accelerated once gravity gave him help on the downward stretch. He glanced behind again at the bottom of the hill and Jay was twenty-five yards behind. He had started to slow and was only running at a fast jog. Nowhere near fast enough to catch up. Bobby hadn't even checked the time on his watch, but he still had a lot of strength. He hadn't thought about Angela once, or the deliveries. He flew around the corner into Clonliffe Road, nearly crashing into the traffic lights. He was getting tired. He pretended in his head that Jay was catching him. He decided not to look round again. Three hundred metres to go. Lungs burning. Legs on fire. Head spinning. Anto told him that this was the time to try and relax.

'Tension makes you run slower.'

He relaxed as much as he could and fell over the crack across the path that denoted the finish line. He was breathing heavier than he had ever done before. He looked at his watch. 8:20. He felt elated. He looked back for Jay. No sign. He walked back down Clonliffe Road, half hoping to bump into Angela. His head was spinning so much that he didn't think he would be able to talk to her. He was pouring with sweat. He sat against the wall of his house. Now all he had to do was to get Jay to keep his side of the deal.

CHAPTER 10

Bobby waited for Jay to call for him but he never did. He played keepie-uppies on the street and thought about where they would dump the drugs. He was determined to make Jay call for him. They could both be stubborn when they wanted. He kicked the ball down Sackville Avenue, ran after it and pretended he was Jay kicking it back to Bobby. He saw Willo follow Git out of the unknown house. Git walked towards Ballybough Road and Willo walked towards Bobby. He had a stare in his eyes and he looked like a zombie.

'Your friend is in our house. Tell him thanks,' mumbled Willo.

'For what?'

Willo didn't answer. He stumbled up Sackville Avenue after his brother. Bobby ran past him and tried to get in the window as quick as he could. He peeled back the corrugated iron and could immediately see a pair of Adidas runners. He knew who they belonged to.

'Jay.'

There was no response. He was lying on the ground.

'Wake up, wake up.'

Jay was lying on his side. Bobby turned him onto his back. The left-hand side of his face was red from being on the cold floorboards. His head was floppy. He opened Jay's eyes and couldn't see his pupils. Bobby was getting worried. He went into the kitchen. The white sink was covered in green and brown grime. There was a nostril piercing, rancid smell. He tiptoed around unidentifiable rubbish to get into the bathroom. The toilet was blocked and was filled up with filth. He couldn't find anything to fill with water, so he clasped his hands together and filled them. Some of it dribbled onto the floor as he made his way over to Jay, the rest he emptied on his head and face. He repeated the process three times before Jay started to move.

'Are you all right?'

Jay mumbled something back. Bobby noticed vomit on the floor a few yards away. Jay had some on his T-shirt. Bobby could see the spoon that he had seen Willo using. It was black and had a needle lying beside it. There was also a roll of tin foil in the corner.

'Jay, are you all right?'

He opened his eyes and they looked like they had been under the chlorinated water of Sean Mac for ages. They were as red as Bobby's Liverpool shirt.

'What have you done?'

'Nothing,' Jay mumbled in a barely audible tone.

'Nothing? You're like a corpse.'

Bobby put his hand on Jay's arm. It was freezing.

'Did you use a needle?'

'They were laughing at me.'

'About what?'

'He said I would go to heaven and come back again.'

'You're back, you're back. Wake up. Don't close your eyes.'

'He said I'd see my da.'

'Your da is in prison.'

'I saw him in the sky when I went to heaven.'

If that's what drugs did to you, Bobby knew he would never be touching them. He couldn't understand why Jay would go anywhere near Willo and Git. They were the losers that Bobby and Jay swore they would never become. *They* had dreams. Jay was a brilliant boxer, probably better than Bobby. He had more skill, but less determination. Anto said he would be a champion. Bobby was angry, sad and tearful but he knew he had to do something.

'Is your ma at home?'

Jay started to nod off again.

'Will I take you home?'

'I want to stay here.'

Bobby knew he couldn't leave him but he didn't know if he could get Jay out the window.

'I'm going to get you a can of Pepsi.'

Bobby was worried Willo might arrive back and do something to Jay. He sprinted like a million dollars depended on it. He got a Pepsi and was back in record time. Jay hadn't moved an inch. His eyes were closed again.

Bobby had a technique to stop the can exploding after shaking. Half pull the lid up and let it bang off the top of the can. He did it seven times. The can opened without a drop spilling. He sat Jay up against the wall. He made him sip the can of Pepsi until every drop was gone.

'You have to promise me you'll never do that again.'

'Where's Willo?'

'You need to get out of here before he gets back. Are you going to promise me?'

'I feel weird, what do I look like?'

'You look like a fucking eejit. You're a spa for doing that.'

'Don't tell Anto.'

'I won't tell anyone.'

Jay couldn't stand up straight when he eventually made it out of the window. He walked to his flat hunched over like the flying-saucer lady. Bobby stayed with him until he was well enough for a shower. He helped him undress. He sat in the bath and Bobby held the shower head over him.

'Is it hot enough?'

'It's nice.'

'Will you promise me you will never go into the unknown house again?'

'I promise.'

He kept the water as hot as Jay could take it. He kept feeling his arm to see if he was getting warmth back in his bones. It would make his life so much easier in the mornings if he had a shower. He wondered when he would stop wetting the bed. His mam told him he would grow out of it, but she had been saying that for years. He dried Jay and sat him on the edge of the bed.

'I need to go asleep.'

'Will I stay with you?'

'No.'

'I'm not leaving you on your own.'

'Please, I'll be grand.'

Bobby left Jay to sleep and kicked a ball against the wall of the pramsheds. It had graffiti all over it. The biggest letters spelt out H-BLOCK. He aimed for the H eleven times in a row, followed by the B, until he had kicked the ball sixty-six times against the wall. He had another sixty quid saved under the carpet from Anto's deliveries. He decided he was going to give it all to the parking fines man. He was sick of losing money in the bookies.

'Sixty pounds!'

The fines man was surprised at the amount.

'My dad won it on the horses.'

'Another winning bet, sure he'll have it paid off in no time.'

He hid the receipt with all the others. He totalled them up. Two hundred and fifty pounds.

Bobby knew Jay hadn't knocked for him because he was embarrassed about what had happened in the unknown house. Two days seemed like an eternity. Two days of torture for Bobby. He wanted to call for Jay but couldn't. He didn't want to be chasing after him, and he wanted to avoid Anto. He had to go to boxing training if he wanted to fight in the All-Ireland, but he wanted Jay to call for him. He had kicked the ball off the H-Block about ten thousand times, hoping Jay would walk down Sackville Avenue and join him. He would pretend he was taking a penalty in the World Cup final. He tried to imagine what the pressure would be like. He never doubted he would score if the time came. He knew what nerves were like after everything he had been through. Jay overcame his nerves by thinking of something else. Bobby would do the same when he got to the World Cup final. He would pretend he was in Ballybough. He would pretend there was an H in the left corner of the goal and he would blast the shot. The crowd would go mad, all cheering his name.

'Bob-by. Bob-by.'

He could hear it was Jay cheering his name. All of a sudden, two hands appeared on the top of the wall. Bobby held the ball. The hands disappeared. Then Jay's big smiling head appeared over the top. He pulled himself up and sat on the wall, dangling his legs on the H and the B. Bobby kicked the ball at him and ran over and grabbed his leg, pretending to pull him down. Instead, he climbed up his leg onto the wall.

'I'm sorry, and thanks for finding me,' Jay said.

'I told you I was faster than you.'

Bobby didn't want to express the emotions he was really feeling because Jay would call him a spa. He was just happy he was back.

'I don't know what would have happened if you hadn't found me.'

'The rats would have got you and eaten your toes, followed by your willy, if they could have found it.'

Jay pushed Bobby off the wall and jumped down himself.

'Do you want to go up to the college?'

The two of them walked up the lanes to the college. They strolled past the open front gate, climbed up the electricity box and scaled the wall. They argued about how many times they had jumped off it. Bobby reckoned it was five hundred. Jay thought it was a thousand. They usually had a plan to rob an orchard, or make a raft, or climb a tree, or bonk into Tolka Park. They had no plan, so they just strolled, and chatted in a boyish way about what would happen if they lost each other. Bobby laughed about the time they became blood brothers, remembering when they had scraped their initials into their arms with a dirty blade they had found in the yard of the paper factory. Jay had jumped off the roof of the paper factory the same day. He had been afraid to do the dangerous ledge walk that was twenty feet above the river. So he had jumped off the roof, which was two storeys high. Bobby thought he was a lunatic for doing it.

'Will we do my jump?' asked Jay.

'Are you mad?'

'Come on, chicken.'

'I'm not doing it; calling me a chicken won't make a difference.'

'Chicken, chicken, chicken.'

'Saying it three times won't make me do it either.'

'Come on, I'll jump first.'

'OK.'

Bobby laughed, knowing that he would let Jay jump and then take the easy way down.

'We have to do it together, then, because if I jump first, you will bottle it.'

Bobby hated it when Jay said he would bottle things. He never did. Just Jay saying it made him even more determined. And Jay knew it did.

They climbed up the back wall of the paper factory and ran across the roof. It wasn't a flat roof. It had two triangles. Up, down, up, down and they were at the edge of a jump that only Jay had ever done. He said it didn't hurt, but Bobby slagged him about walking funny for two weeks afterwards.

'Hold hands and we'll jump together,' said Jay.

'I'm not holding your hand.'

'Come on!'

'OK, on the count of three.'

'On three, or after three?'

'What do you mean?'

'Is it one, two, three, go? Or is it one, two, three jump? Do we jump on go, or do we jump on three?'

'What are you talking about? You say, one, two, three and when you say three, we'll jump.'

'On three or after three?'

'One, two, threeeeeeeeeeeeeeeeeeeeeeeeeeeee.'

They landed with a loud thump, stumbling out onto the road. They stood up and looked at each other.

'Are your feet stinging?'

'No, are yours?'

'No.'

They both knew the other was lying. They burst out laughing.

'Do you still think we're different?' asked Bobby.

'When did I say that?'

'You said I was a poshie.'

'I was only joking with you.'

'I'm not a poshie.'

'I know. Isn't your da in the Sunset every day?'

'So, we are the same?'

'You're my best friend in the whole world.'

Bobby always wanted Jay to say that to him. He was envious of Jay living in the flats. He had a real claim on being a Ballybough boy. Bobby pretended he was from the flats.

'I lied to you about something.'

Bobby immediately got the worried feeling again. He wanted everything to be the way it was before they ever delivered a video for Anto.

'You had your secret about wetting the bed.'

'What's your secret?'

'My da isn't in prison.'

'Where is he?'

'Glasnevin.'

'He lives in Glasnevin? That's only up the road.'

'He's buried in Glasnevin, you dope.'

Bobby didn't know what to say. It was a strange secret to have.

'He's dead, Bobby.'

'Why did you say he was in prison?'

'I don't know.'

Bobby was afraid to ask how he had died. Jay didn't tell him.

'Anto asked us to knock down before boxing.'

Bobby didn't want to mention Anto's name. He was hoping the deliveries would stop.

'I'll knock for you after my dinner,' he said reluctantly.

'Where have you been for the past two days?' asked Anto. 'Jay has had to do deliveries on his own. I want the two of you doing it together.'

Jay had failed to mention doing deliveries on his own.

'Take this up to Micka. He'll be at the pool in fifteen minutes.'

'We could jog it in five. Well I could, I don't know about Jay.'

'Don't be hanging around there too long. He'll be there at seven on the button.'

'How many deliveries did you do on your own?'

'Twenty in two days. I think that's a hundred quid.'

'You're getting good at maths. There's no way you did twenty deliveries.'

'Ah, no, it was just one to Micka and one to Johnny.'

Bobby got a knot in his stomach. Jay had lost the race and he was still delivering.

'You lost the race.'

'What could I say to Anto?'

'Did you go back to the unknown house?'

'No.'

'You're a liar.'

'How do you know?'

'I know by the look on your face. Am I going to find you on the floor again?'

'No. Let's go.'

Jay sprinted off. Bobby tucked in behind him and watched the video in Jay's left hand. He could see that Jay's knuckles were white he was gripping it so hard. It was like a relay baton in his hand. He could feel Jay slowing down as they passed the Sunset. He came up alongside him and then jogged two yards past. He wanted to turn around and do what Eamonn Coghlan had done in 1983. He couldn't do it, though. He slowed to Jay's pace. Bobby could hear him breathing harder than he normally would.

'Are you all right?'

'Just not as fit as you.'

'Let's walk together the rest of the way.'

The handover of the cassette was like a smooth relay change. Jay gave it to Micka. Not a word was exchanged.

Anto was already at the boxing club collecting subs from all the boxers when Jay and Bobby arrived. They still had to pay subs, but Anto didn't fine them the five pence for being late. Bobby knew there was a vibe between himself and Jay, and he thought Anto could see it too. He could feel Anto staring at him. He felt his every movement was being watched.

'The All-Ireland final is on next week. How are you feeling?'

'Fine.'

'Bobby, if there is ever anything worrying you, you know you can talk to me.'

'OK.'

'Is there anything worrying you?'

'Like what?'

'If I knew what, I wouldn't be asking, would I?'

Anto stared at him for longer than normal. Bobby thought he had an intensity of a stare that could look into his brain.

'I want you to fight Jay in sparring tonight. I want you to think it is the All-Ireland final. There will be hundreds of people there. Concentrate tonight on blocking out everything outside the ring. No taking it easy. I want you to punch him harder than you have ever done before. Do you understand?'

Bobby nodded his head. He had never fought Jay like it was the All-Ireland final. Sparring was different to competition. You never went flat out in sparring, or threw your hardest punches. Especially at your best friend.

Bobby climbed into the ring. He looked across to see Anto putting Jay's gumshield in. He slapped him on the side of the headguard and shouted one final instruction. He called them into the centre of the ring.

'Touch gloves.'

They looked each other in the eye.

'Good luck,' offered Bobby.

'You're going to need it,' laughed Jay, who was relishing the change in rules.

Bobby knew he'd better get serious. He stepped towards Jay with his hands close to his face. Jay swung a punch at Bobby's ribs and winded him slightly. He tried to punch Bobby in the head, but he couldn't get through his gloves. Bobby remembered Anto always telling him to relax. *Relax when running, relax when boxing. Your feet get lighter when you're relaxed, enabling you to move faster.* He relaxed and could feel himself moving quicker. He threw a quick right-left combination that he had been practising in the mirror at home. The right punch hit Jay's right glove. It moved it enough to give

Bobby a clear shot at the head. He rocked Jay with the left hook more than he had ever done before. He quickly pounced and hit Jay with a flurry of punches, knocking him to the canvas. Anto told him to block out the outside noises but he couldn't. All the lads in the club were getting closer to the ring, shouting all sorts of encouragement for both of them. Anto told him if he could hear noises, he wasn't in the zone. Jay ran at him after Anto wiped the top of his gloves on his shirt. He threw as many punches as he could. Bobby easily got out of the way. He felt like Jay's punches were moving in slow motion. He saw a gap in Jay's guard and landed a fierce right hand, flush on Jay's nose. It rocked Jay back a few steps. Normally that meant an eight-second count, but Anto said 'fight on'. A trickle of blood started to meander towards Jay's lip. He tasted it with the tip of his tongue, and then started to feel angry. Bobby felt calm, surprisingly calm. He couldn't hear any noises again. Jay ran at him, swinging wildly. Bobby moved sideways to avoid Jay's punches, then, when he saw the moment to pounce, he nailed Jay again with a left hook. He followed it with a right and another left. Jay slipped back onto the canvas, landing on his bum.

'Right, that's enough. Headguards off in the corner.'

Anto undid the strap that held the sweaty head-guards in place.

'What lesson did you learn, Jay?'

'Nothing.'

'You're pissed off, are you?'

Jay was stubborn when he wanted to be. Bobby had a big smile on the inside that he kept there. He didn't want to show any emotion.

'I must have never mentioned the word technique before.'

Anto looked at Jay. He wasn't getting a response.

'Bobby, you're ready for next week. The last All-Ireland winner from this club was me.'

'You've told us a hundred times.'

'Jay, you need to learn a lesson from tonight. Or you will have no chance next week. You should be pissed off. That performance was an embarrassment.'

Bobby didn't mention the video on the way home because he knew Jay was pissed off about losing the fight. Bobby felt on top of the world. The winning feeling was matched by no other. Normally, Bobby would have a tingle of excitement in his stomach for days after a win. He would picture the fight and the punches landed. Hitting Jay was different though. He was glad he won, but it didn't give him the same satisfaction. It gave him confidence; Jay was a weight above him. He was going to win the All-Ireland.

Willo and Git jumped down from the wall of the bridge when they saw the boys coming. Willo was jumping up and down on the spot like he was freezing in the winter. It was a beautiful summer's evening.

'What do they want?' asked Bobby.

'How would I know?'

'You're their best friend.'

Willo walked towards them with his hands still in his pockets.

'Jay, have you got any more of that stuff? The same as last night.'

'Last night, Jay?'

'You shut your mouth or I'll kick in your door again,' Willo sneered at Bobby. 'I've fifty quid,' he said to Jay.

Willo took his hands out of his pockets. He had two piles of fifty pence pieces.

'Did you rob an amusement arcade?'

'Take it.'

'I'm not taking your poxy change.'

Jay whispered something at Willo that Bobby couldn't hear. Willo motioned at Git and the two of them scurried down the hill towards the flats. Bobby stared at him.

'Piss off. It's better than throwing it away.'

'You promised we'd dump it.'

'You can give it to the parking fines man.'

Jay took two twenty pound notes and one tenner out of his pocket.

'Here. I don't want it.'

'I don't want it either.'

Jay dropped it on the ground and started walking down the hill.

'I'm not picking it up.'

'Neither am I.'

Bobby looked at the money on the ground. He couldn't leave it there. He grabbed it and ran down the hill after Jay.

'I don't want the money. I just want you back.'

'What?'

'You know what I mean.'

'I haven't gone anywhere.'

'You've changed. You made promises and didn't keep them.'

'It's not my fault. What can we say to Anto?'

'We can tell him we know and we're stopping.'

'I'm not telling him.'

'I'm going to tell him.'

'Tell him what?'

'That we know what's in them.'

'How do we know what's in them?'

'Cause you opened it.'

'You're going to rat on me?'

'Yeah.'

'Rat then. Rat face.'

He turned his back on Bobby and walked away.

After a few strides, he turned back and returned for his money. He stared at Bobby without saying a word. Bobby backed onto the steps of the derelict three-storey house. It was their favourite house for catching pigeons. Jay was the master, Bobby his apprentice. There was no upper floor, just wooden beams. Jay would crawl along them, backing the pigeons into a corner. He was the master bird handler. The pigeons never panicked when Jay held them. He was able to handle them gently, but he was always in control.

CHAPTER 11

Bobby prayed like he had never prayed before. He said twenty-five Our Fathers, even adding on the extra bit he'd learned, that only Protestants said. He said twenty-five Hail Marys, picturing her looking after Jay every time. He prayed that their friendship would go back to the way it was.

The loud bang on the door woke him. He sat upright in bed. He heard his dad running down the stairs. It was still pitch dark, so Bobby knew it was before four-thirty. It got bright then, but the sun didn't start shining on Croke Park until just after half seven.

'Have you seen Jason?' Bernie said loudly enough for the whole house to hear her.

Bobby's mam came out in her dressing-gown.

'Is everything OK, Miss McCann?'

'Jason didn't come home last night. I'm really worried about him. Have you any idea where he might be?'

Jay's mam never knocked on Bobby's hall door. So Bobby knew something was wrong.

She never called him Jason either.

'Come in, Bernie.'

Laura put an arm around her shoulder and told her to calm down.

'Everything will be OK.'

She put on the kettle while Bobby explained they had been to boxing and came home together, omitting the fight they had had and the meeting with Willo and Git.

Bobby thought straight away that Jay was probably lying on the floor of the unknown house.

'He might have fallen asleep in Anto's, watching videos. Will I run down and check for you?'

He couldn't think of anything else to say.

'You can't be knocking on his door this late,' said his mam.

'Of course he can, love. Run down quickly, Bobby,' ordered his dad.

Bobby flew up the stairs and put his runners on with no socks. He grabbed his Liverpool shirt from its hanging place on the side of the top bunk and raced down the stairs. He took off down Foster Terrace, passing Anto's without stopping, flew out onto Ballybough Road, and was outside the unknown house in record time. He was completely out of breath. He didn't know whether he wanted Jay to be inside or not. He peeled back the corrugated iron and looked inside. He could see two people asleep on the couch and another person slumped against the wall. He looked for Jay's Adidas runners. No sign. He climbed inside and Willo stirred.

'Is Jay here?'

He pointed towards the bathroom. Bobby walked towards the door slowly, the fear in his stomach growing. He didn't see Jay until he looked in the bath. He had vomit down the front of his T-shirt and blood on the inside of his left arm. The bathroom had the worst smell imaginable. The fact that the toilet was blocked didn't help. He couldn't understand why Jay was in the bath. His trousers were unzipped and Bobby could see he had no underpants on. He could see the small amount of pubic hair that Jay had. Bobby had slagged him over it, as he was the first to get any. He had pulled his first one out when he'd got it and waved it around in the air before throwing it at Bobby. Maybe he'd wiped his ass with his underpants. Bobby thought that wasn't a bad idea because newspaper slid the poo across your bum. They had used newspaper on the tracks or the canal bank at some stage. It was better than trekking all the way home. He tried to make Jay sit up, but he was like a dead weight. There was no way he could pull him out of the bath. Bobby took Jay's vomit-stained T-shirt off and put his Liverpool shirt on him. He rolled up the vomit-soaked one and put it between Jay's head and the bath, clean side facing out. Jay's eyes stayed closed. Bobby slapped his face. No response. He did it again, though, even harder. Still no response. He thought about feeling for a pulse, but he wasn't sure what to do.

Now was the time to tell Anto. The voice in his head told him to. He felt like he was floating out of the unknown house, looking at the drug-fuelled bodies as he passed. None of them stirred. He found himself out on the street. He legs started moving on their own. He was sprinting flat out. Bang, bang, bang.

The lights came on in Anto's house. Bobby could see his silhouette moving slowly towards the door. He put his eye up to the glass and could tell it was Bobby straight away. He had the words 'what's wrong' out before the door even opened.

'It's Jay. I can't wake him.'

'What do you mean? Where is he?'

'In the unknown house.'

Anto put two and two together and had his trousers and runners on in no time. He sprinted down the road. Bobby couldn't keep up. Anto was in the window before Bobby got there. He could hear the screams.

'Where is he? Where is he?'

Bobby was pushed out of the way by an escaping Willo. He was followed out by Git and Gringo. Gringo gave him a stare with pupils so large they took over his whole eye. They looked like black snooker balls. Anto already had Jay out of the bath when Bobby arrived. He was feeling for a pulse.

'We need to call an ambulance,' Bobby said quietly.

'I'll go and call one. You stay here.'

'What will I do?'

'Just mind him, he's going to be all right,' said Anto, panicked.

'His mam is in my house.'

'Stay here and mind him, I'll be back in a minute,' Anto ordered him.

Bobby held Jay's hand. It was much warmer than before. He could see the outline of the JMcC Jay had scraped into his arm. Bobby had scraped BR into his arm.

'Do you remember that day, Jay,' Bobby whispered. 'I touched my BR off your JMcC? You moaned for a week about having to scrape more initials into your arm. We'll go swimming in the Tolka next week. I have to get a massive head start if we're racing though.'

Bobby looked down at Jay's fly. He reached down and pulled it up. He closed the button and then gently placed Jay's head on the top of his leg. He put his hand on Jay's cheek and squeezed it gently with his thumb and forefinger. He could see the fluff on his upper lip that Jay claimed was stubble. Bobby had slagged him, saying it was just bum fluff. Bobby hated the thought of hair growing on his face. And on his legs. He leaned down and kissed Jay on the forehead. It was a very gentle kiss.

'Please God make him better.'

The calm was interrupted by the noise Anto made coming back in the window.

'The ambulance is on the way,' Anto said, as he picked Jay up and carried him over to the window.

The noise of the ambulance arriving took over the conversation.

'Hold the window back.'

Bobby did as he was told. Anto was able to get Jay out without too much trouble. He held Jay in his arms. The ambulance turned into Sackville Avenue much more slowly than Bobby expected. The blue lights lit up the flats every half-second of their turn. When they saw Anto they turned the siren off but the lights kept flashing.

'What's wrong?'

'I think it might be heroin,' responded Anto.

The ambulance men lifted Jay straight into the back of the ambulance. One of them started to feel his neck, then his wrist. He shouted at his colleague, who started rooting in his bag for something.

'Are you this child's father?'

'Em… no not quite. I'm his… eh, coach.'

'Are you coming with him?'

Bobby stared at him while waiting for an answer.

'Em… where are you taking him?'

'Temple Street Hospital.'

They didn't give Anto any more time to think. The ambulance sped off down Sackville Avenue without him, passing Bobby's house on the way to the hospital.

'Is he going to be OK?' asked Bobby.

'He should be, he should be.'

Anto suddenly grabbed Bobby by the arm. He held it so tight Bobby could feel knuckles sticking into the side of his rib cage. The pain of each knuckle digging into him made his whole body sting with pain. He knew what was coming next. He knew whose fault everything was. He knew the one person he couldn't tell the truth to was Anto.

'What happened last week? You need to tell me everything. Starting with the robbery.'

'We should tell Bernie.'

Anto squeezed even tighter, causing the pain to sting behind Bobby's eyes. He released the grip completely and put his arm gently around Bobby's shoulders.

'All I want is the truth.'

'Willo said if he tried it, he would go to heaven and see his da.'

'You heard him say that?'

'No, I wasn't there. I found him there. I cleaned

him up. He promised never to go back.'

'And that's it?'

'He was pissed off I beat him in the ring. I left him at the top of the road and he said he was going home.'

'When did you find him the first time?'

'Last week.'

'Before or after the video was robbed.'

'After.'

'OK, OK. You came to get me because you were scared. I'll look after you. You won't get in trouble.'

Anto patted him on the back of the head, the same way he would after a good round sparring.

'Everything's going to be all right. Don't worry.'

Bobby told them all what he knew about the unknown house and how Jay had told him about the junkies. He didn't tell them about finding him in there the first time. He said he didn't know if he had taken anything. He was thinking up answers on the spot, and his little lies were leading to bigger ones. There was no mention of videos, so the real truth couldn't come out. Anto told Bernie not to worry, that the ambulance man said everything was going to be OK. Anto was a brilliant liar, but now Bobby could see straight through him.

Bernie left for the hospital with his mam. Anto stayed talking to his dad, explaining what he knew about the scumbags, Willo and Git. Bobby was allowed to listen to some of the stories his dad told about how the area had changed. Then he was sent to bed.

He lay in bed touching every 'Jay' that was written under the laths of the top bunk. He had written it sixteen times. Once on each lath. There were 128 'Bobbys'. He listened to the door closing when Anto left. He listened to his dad going to bed. He listened to Kevin's heavy breathing. He heard the door of the taxi close when his mam came home. He heard her put the key in the latch really quietly. She tried to sneak into the hall. Bobby was sitting on the stairs waiting for her.

'Is he OK?'

She walked towards him without speaking. She pulled his head into her belly and squeezed. He heard the tears. She got down on her hunkers and put his cheek next to hers. He could feel each tear dropping from her eye.

'I'm glad you're OK.'

'Is Jay OK?'

'He should be. They will know more tomorrow. Go up to bed and say a few prayers.'

Listening to his mam and dad talking was frustrating for Bobby. The bedroom wall wasn't thick enough to block out all the noise. He could hear a murmur and, every once in a while, he could make out a whole word. Not enough to understand what they were talking about. Loud enough, though, to take his mind off everything that was happening. He knew a line of questioning was going to start first thing in the morning. He knew he couldn't tell them the whole truth. He couldn't tell anyone the truth any more.

CHAPTER 12

Bobby didn't sleep long enough to wet the bed. His mam said she hadn't slept at all. Bobby made her a strong cup of coffee while she sat at the dining-room table in her dressing-gown. She always used the free Nescafé cup she had got with the extra large jar of finely ground coffee. Bobby loved the smell, but hated the taste. She always drank more coffee when she was stressed.

Anto never drank coffee, or tea. Matt said he was the only man who had ever refused a cup of tea in his home. He had never knocked on Bobby's door at nine in the morning, especially in a pair of running shorts.

'I was just anxious to hear if there was news from the hospital last night.'

'I stayed with Bernie until six. They said they would know more today. I said I'd go back up this morning.'

'I'm going on a run. I thought it might take Bobby's mind off things.'

'I don't want to go.'

'Of course you do,' his dad told him. 'Don't keep him waiting,'

Bobby changed into his shorts and T-shirt. He didn't want to go anywhere with Anto ever again. He felt really small beside him. Two of his legs didn't even make up the width of one of Anto's.

'Where will we start?'

'I normally start at the Fluther Good pub.'

'Why don't we start at the top of the road and finish there too?'

Bobby didn't care where he started. He reset his stopwatch.

'Are you timing yourself?'

'Yeah, I always do.'

'What's your record?'

'Not as fast as you.'

'I never time myself.'

'It's eight minutes.'

'OK, if you beat it, I'll give you a tenner.'

Bobby knew he shouldn't have lied. He could hear his mam's voice in his head, saying, 'The truth always comes out at some stage!'

'I meant eight minutes twenty.'

'Yeah, right!'

Anto showed him a few new stretches he could do for his hamstrings. Bobby loved the feeling stretching gave him. Anto was a stickler for warming-up properly. At boxing, he would make them warm-up for half an hour before they were even allowed to hit the punch-bag.

'Let's do a light jog and then we'll start.'

'Is that not wasted energy? You just don't want to give me the tenner.'

'It'll make you run faster.'

When they got to the start, Anto said to follow his lead. Bobby never started as fast, not even when he outran Jay. The uphill stretch into Summerhill Parade came much quicker and Bobby's legs were burning already. Anto could hear him breathing heavily, as there was no conversation.

'Big deep breaths, in your nose and out your mouth.'

Bobby followed the instructions. They flew around the corner at the Sunset. Bobby looked at his watch, but they were going much faster than normal and Bobby couldn't see the exact time.

'Don't look at the time. Stay focused. Keep the breathing going.'

Anto sounded like he was in the boxing club. He was brilliant at giving the right instructions. Bobby always gave it that little bit extra for him. When they turned the corner behind Croke Park, Anto told him to get a breather on the downhill stretch behind the Hogan Stand. Bobby was determined to keep up. He knew Anto could run faster.

'I think I'm going to have to stop,' Bobby got

out, despite the fact that his lungs were burning like never before and his legs felt like jelly.

'Concentrate on your breathing. We're nearly there.'

Bobby knew in his head that he wasn't going to give up. He was going to beat eight minutes for Jay. If he beat his record, Jay was going to come back fitter than ever. If he didn't, then he didn't know what was going to happen. Bobby came up with scenarios like this all the time. He would make deals with God that if he stopped wetting the bed, his dad would stop drinking. If he stopped wetting the bed, he would never curse again. He knew he couldn't keep some of the promises, but he made them anyway. He always talked to God before he went to sleep. God never answered him. He was never going to stop wetting the bed. He would never be able to get married, because he would pee on his wife in the middle of the night. He normally didn't have thoughts like this when he was running. It must be the effort he was putting in.

When they got to the off-licence on Clonliffe Road, the pain became enjoyable. No matter how sore his legs were, he always had energy left to sprint near the end. That is what would win him an Olympic gold. Bobby picked up the pace. He turned right into Ballybough Road. Just the flats to run past and they were home. He picked up the pace again. Each time, Anto stayed alongside him. One hundred yards to go. Fifty yards to go. Bobby collapsed onto the ground and could feel his knees cutting as he landed. He turned over on his back and felt for the stop button on his watch. He was breathing so heavily that he couldn't open his eyes.

'Try and sit up, the blood will all rush to your head,' said Anto, hardly sounding out of breath.

Bobby followed the order and looked at his knees. Both were bleeding, but there was no pain. Bobby knew he had beaten eight minutes thirty. He was afraid to look at the watch.

'What time did you do?' asked Anto.

He looked at the watch.

7:59.74.

He wiped his eyes and looked again. The time didn't change. He couldn't believe it.

'Seven minutes fifty-nine seconds,' said a panting Bobby.

'Brilliant. That was an easy tenner for you,' said Anto, not knowing how Bobby felt inside.

'We'll walk for a few minutes to cool down. Let's walk down the avenue and back again.'

Just as he said 'the avenue', Bobby realised that he hadn't thought about Jay much in the previous seven minutes and fifty-nine seconds. The thoughts started coming thick and fast. What could he do to make everything better again? He started to think everything was his fault.

'I don't want to have to ask this question, because I trust you like you are my little brother. My dreams are about you winning that All-Ireland title, maybe even going to box in the Olympics.'

'I want to run in the Olympics.'

'And you can if you want. You are going to be good enough, to box or run.'

Anto leaned down and looked Bobby in the eye. He put one hand gently on his shoulder. He put the other on the side of his face. It felt warm against his bare cheek.

'Look me in the eye… Was the video robbed?'

Bobby didn't hesitate with an answer.

'Exactly the way we told you. Jay got a bloody nose because of that video.'

Anto kept looking in his eyes. All Bobby could think was not to blink as Jay said it made you the loser in a staring match.

'Go on home. I'll call for you on the way to boxing.'

Bobby was thinking in his head that he wasn't going boxing, but he decided to say nothing. He felt comfortable telling lies to Anto because the truth would lead to more problems.

'Did you know Jay was using heroin?' asked his mam.

'No, but I knew that they did it in the unknown house.'

'Right on our doorstep there are people using heroin.'

Laura looked at Matt in absolute disgust.

'And our thirteen-year old son knows about it.'

'It's a disgrace. It's destroying our city,' added Matt.

'It will destroy our family if we stay in this area.'

'We're not leaving,' shouted Bobby, as if his opinion mattered.

Bobby was sitting against the H-Block wall when he saw the navy blue Nissan Bluebird pull up outside his house. Everyone knew the undercover cops drove them; it made them whatever the opposite of undercover was. Overcover, thought Bobby. One of them stood with his hand in his pockets, while the other one knocked on the door. He saw an arm reach out to shake hands but he couldn't tell if it was his mam's or dad's. He thought about disappearing for a while but he knew he couldn't run forever. He would have to tell them what had happened, even though Jay would call him a rat.

Matt didn't have to shout for him. He saw Bobby looking his way and called him with a hand signal. He waited for him, attempting to pick him up when he was within arm's reach. Bobby pushed him away, not wanting to be treated like a baby.

'This is Detective McNeill and Detective Burns,' said Matt.

McNeill stood up and offered his hand to shake. Bobby reached out and received what Anto would call a weak handshake. McNeill hardly touched his hand, just shaking the top of Bobby's fingers. 'Hold that hand and squeeze,' Anto would tell them, 'it's a sign of strength.'

'Firstly, Bobby, we would like to tell you that you are not in trouble. Somebody gave Jason heroin,' McNeill announced, acting concerned.

'Jay.'

'Sorry, Jay. We are not sure where he got it. We thought that, as you were his best friend, he might have said something to you.'

Bobby could see that McNeill was going to do all the talking and Burns was going to stay quiet and take notes.

'Like what?'

'Something to do with drugs or knowing someone who was selling heroin.'

'I think I know where he got it.'

Bobby knew Jay would never have touched the stuff if it wasn't for Willo Brown and the unknown house.

'What did you say?'

'I think I know where he got it.'

'Where?'

'Number six, Sackville Avenue. We call it the unknown house.'

'How do you know?'

'Because I found Jay in there.'

Detective Burns was scribbling furiously.

'Keep talking, Bobby.'

'What else can I say?'

'When did you find him?'

'I found him the other day. All the junkies use it.'

'What junkies?'

Bobby could see Burns was struggling to keep up with the pace. Like Jay on their last run to the swimming pool.

'Willo and Git Brown. They made him do it, it's their fault.'

'How many times was he in the house?'

'I found Jay there once before last night. He was passed out on the floor. I brought him home and made sure he was OK.'

'How did you even think to look there?'

'Willo told me he was there.'

'And this Willo fella, where does he live?'

'He lives in the flats, but he's always in the unknown house.'

'And Jay told you that Willo gave him heroin?'

'Yeah. Willo and Git.'

The two detectives went outside to talk. Bobby

could feel his mam and dad seething. Bobby knew he had just made their minds up about leaving Ballybough.

'Why didn't you tell us?' asked his mother, who had a look of sadness and anger all in one stare.

'I didn't want him getting into trouble.'

'He was already in trouble. You could have saved him from getting into more trouble.'

Bobby knew he was partly responsible. He could have done something, but he thought he was doing the right thing by staying quiet. Detective McNeill came back in to thank Bobby and his parents.

'We'll be back to talk to you again.'

'Thank you, detective,' said his mam.

They managed a smile at each other.

Boy, 13, in a coma after heroin overdose

Bobby knew that when somebody was in a coma it meant they were really sick. He never expected that Jay's story would be on the front of the *Evening Press*, because he didn't realise that Jay was really sick. Anto had said he would be all right, and he was sure his mam had said that Jay would be all right. The story didn't mention Jay's name, it just called him a boy from the inner city. Anto convinced Matt that it would be best if Bobby did some extra training in the club to take his mind off things. Anto gave him one-on-one coaching, refusing to let him spar before his big fight. Normally, he would be nervous leading up to a club fight. He expected to be ten times as nervous leading up to the biggest fight of his life, but he couldn't get nervous as much as he tried. There was something huge missing from the build-up.

Going to training with Anto was not the same as going with Jay. There was never a moment of silence between Bobby and his best friend, they just talked and talked. Anto walked with him and hardly said a thing. Just the odd comment that required short answers from Bobby. It wasn't a real conversation. Bobby didn't know how Anto felt.

'The police called to my house,' said Bobby, surprising Anto with the comment.

'The police. What did they want to know?'

'How Jay got the heroin.'

'What did you say?'

'I told them the truth. He went to the unknown house and Willo gave it to him.'

'I have been searching high and low for Willo, but he seems to have disappeared. I will find him though, and when I do…'

'Will he get in trouble?'

'He'll get in more trouble if I find him before the cops.'

Bobby wanted to see Jay in hospital. His mam didn't think it was a good idea. She made up excuses, none of which Bobby believed. He pleaded with his dad. Sometimes he was easier to convince.

'If you don't let me go I'm not fighting in the final.'

'It will be your loss if you don't fight.'

'You'll get a fright if you see him hooked up to all the machines.'

'It's better than not seeing him at all.'

Temple Street Hospital was only a few hundred yards from Croke Park. When the sun shone, Ballybough looked like the most beautiful place on earth. The swans in the canal looked whiter than white. Bobby's mam had never once walked down the canal in fifteen years of living in Ballybough. She was surprised by the calm beauty of the water. Bobby explained that there were very few fish in that section of the canal. He pointed out the exact spots where fish were likely to be. A large sycamore tree hung out over the water, always looking like it was about to fall.

'All the big fish hide in the shadow,' explained Bobby.

'To get out of the hot sun?'

'No mam, to get away from fishermen's hooks.'

Bobby loved making people laugh. He knew

Jay was going to be asleep but he was still going to make him laugh.

The entrance to Temple Street Hospital was like the front door of a house. The old Georgian building was more modern inside than Bobby imagined. It had the immediate smell of hospital. There were signs for the different wards. Each one was named after a saint. Jay was in St Mark's.

There was a big statue of Jesus in a glass cabinet on the wall. He had a long, red, velvety cape on. Bobby thought he looked more like a superhero.

'Dad, he looks more like Superman.'

The ward sister looked straight down her pointy nose at Bobby.

'That is St Mark.'

She pointed to a plaque on the wall. It had a description of St Mark that Bobby didn't want to read.

'Where is Jay?'

She led them down a short corridor. There were rooms with six beds and rooms with four beds. Jay was in a much smaller room. It had a window that looked directly at the large flats across the road. That was the best view Jay could have wished for. Bobby was a bit tentative. He didn't expect the number of machines and wires, even though he knew they would be there. There was a constant beeping noise. Jay had tubes in both nostrils. His hands were down by his side. Laura held one of them and just looked at him. Bobby put his hand on Jay's arm. He had light blue pyjamas on.

'Thanks for coming, Bobby,' whispered Bernie, as she made her way to the side of the bed.

She held Jay's hand and put her arm around Bobby.

'They said he is stable, which is good news, I suppose.'

'It is, Bernie, it is.'

Laura moved to embrace Bernie. Bobby put his hand on Jay's face.

'I'll be back with the All-Ireland trophy,' Bobby whispered at him.

CHAPTER 13

Bobby had a feeling that he was going to win the fight. His dad told him just to concentrate on relaxing.

'Win the fight and Jay will be OK.'

He believed his dad.

Laura had never been to see Bobby box. She hated it and it took months of protesting from Bobby for her even to allow him to go training.

'Why in God's name would I want to see someone punching my son in the head?'

'You'll be watching me avoiding the punches.'

'I don't want to see you punching anyone in the head either.'

She just didn't get boxing. It disgusted her. She couldn't even watch Barry McGuigan.

To get to the dressing-rooms in the National Boxing Stadium, Bobby had to walk through the main auditorium, where the ring was. He couldn't believe the number of people in the crowd. He knew the stadium capacity was eight thousand. It was about a quarter full. The finals spread out over two days. It started with the lower weights and moved up to the heavier boxers. Bobby looked around the changing-room for his opponent. Anto wanted him to get in the zone. There was no talking while Anto strapped up Bobby's hands. He massaged Bobby's legs to get them loose, then put Deep Heat on them. Bobby loved the smell, even though it stung the inside of his nostrils. Anto took two red vests and two blue vests out of his bag. They had St Francis Boxing Club written on the back. Bobby turned them around to see the front. Two had the initials JMcC on them and two had BR on them. Seeing the initials gave Bobby the nervous knot in his stomach that he thought would have been there all week.

'I'm wearing Jay's vest.'

Anto smiled, knowing that was the decision Bobby was going to make.

'You're fighting for Jay tonight.'

Bobby didn't answer him.

'Stay calm and focused.'

Bobby nodded. He was in the zone and Anto knew it. He talked to him but Bobby didn't really hear what he was saying. Bobby knew what he had to do. He repeated Anto's words over and over in his mind. 'Stay calm and focused.'

'Do you know what you're going to do?' asked Anto.

Bobby nodded again. Defend and counter-punch. That's what he would do for the first minute. Look for his opponent's weaknesses.

'Ryan in the blue corner, fighting Wilson in the red corner. Boxers to the centre of the ring please.'

Bobby stared into his opponent's eyes. He didn't see any fear. Bobby walked forwards with his hands held high. Wilson threw a flurry of punches at Bobby's head, none of which were able to penetrate Bobby's high guard. Bobby bounced on his toes and moved from side to side. He threw a left jab that connected with Wilson's nose. Wilson retaliated with strong lefts and rights that stunned Bobby. He held on to his opponent's arms to get a breather. He knew he had lost the first round. He would have to win the next two to be victorious.

Anto was calm in the corner. He had his routine. Gumshield out. Water in. Three small slugs. First one, gargle it and spit it out. Next two, drink them.

'You need to start throwing more punches. You're one round down. Don't let him throw the first punch. Are you OK?'

Bobby felt a bit sluggish. There was no adrenaline driving him on.

'He's very strong.'

'So are you. But not if you don't try and hit him.'

Anto put Bobby's gumshield in and slapped him on the side of the headguard.

'Do it for Jay.'

Bobby walked out with determination. Only two rounds left. He was going to throw as many punches as he physically could. The bell went for the start of round two, and as he walked forwards, he could see it was Jay walking towards him. He froze and dropped his hands. Wilson hit him harder than he had been ever hit in his life. His head spun as he fell to the canvas. When he got to his feet he could hear the referee saying 'five, six, seven, eight'.

'Are you OK to box on?'

'Yes,' said Bobby, as he held his gloves up to show he was OK.

He walked forward and saw Wilson. He threw a few punches, none of which landed. Wilson sensed he had the fight won. He pushed Bobby away with both gloves, landing a few punches just as the bell sounded.

Anto had a look of disappointment Bobby could understand. He was about to lose without giving it his best. Anto was always able to get the best out of Bobby. Now Bobby was going to let him down. All the years of training, to lose in the final.

'Sit down and listen.'

Bobby sat down and took a deep breath. In his nose and out his mouth.

'You are lucky to be able to fight. Think about what Jay would do to be here now. Go out there and knock him out. He is coming in with his left hand held low. Fake to throw a left, and throw a big right hand.'

'A big right hand.'

Bobby pictured the punch in his head. A knock-out was now his only chance of winning. He stood up from his seat and shook his hands down by his side. His arms were getting tired. He walked to the centre of the ring. Jay walked towards him again.

'Knock me out, Bobby. Knock me out, Bobby.'

Bobby tried to focus on Wilson's left glove. He saw it dropping. He faked a left punch and followed it with a massive right hook. It connected flush on the side of Wilson's head, knocking him straight to the canvas. Bobby was sent to the corner of the ring while the referee counted to eight. Wilson didn't make it to his feet on time. The referee put his arms out to signal the end of the fight. Bobby didn't feel the elation he thought he would. Anto jumped into the ring and lifted him up in the air.

'You did it, you did it.'

The referee approached Bobby and signalled for him to go to the opposing corner to shake hands. He gave Wilson a hug.

'Well done,' said his coach.

'It was a lucky punch.'

The difference between the winner's trophy and the loser's trophy was twelve inches. A photographer took a picture of both boxers holding their marble-bottomed plastic statues. Bobby looked down to see his dad and brother at ringside. Kevin had never seen Bobby fight. It was the first time Bobby had seen him looking proud of one of his achievements.

His dad lifted him up in the air, too, when he came down the steps of the ring.

'Well done,' said Kevin. 'That was some punch.'

'Thanks.'

'Are you coming home with us?'

Bobby looked at Anto.

'I'm going to stay and watch a few fights. I'll go home with Anto.'

His dad didn't object. Bobby put the trophy in his kitbag. It just about fitted. Anto took the tape off his hands and left him on his own to change. Bobby had no intention of staying to watch any more fights. He was going to Temple Street to show Jay his All-Ireland trophy, just like he said he would. He walked into the auditorium and saw Anto talking to one of the white-jacketed referees. He sneaked around the opposite side and walked out into the cool night air, a champion.

Bobby calculated that the run from the National Stadium to Temple Street was seven kilometres. He could jog a kilometre in five minutes without being out of breath. It was quicker to jog than to take the bus. And free.

Temple Street had visiting hours. That meant Bobby had to bonk in. If he could bonk into Dalymount, he knew he could bonk into a hospital that had a front door that was never locked. Jay's motto of not looking suspicious was in his head. Bobby strolled straight past the reception desk, not needing to glance sideways to see a nurse busy scribbling something on a chart. He walked slowly up the wide staircase, holding the mahogany banister for support. It was shining and smelled of fresh polish. Each step creaked, even under Bobby's slight, thirty-one-kilo frame. The marble base had stuck into Bobby's back on the run, but it was only a little bit of pain, so he ignored it.

The noise was gone. The noise of the beeping machine. Jay was lying much lower in the bed. Bobby noticed the tubes were gone. Jay's hands were under the sheet, which was pulled up onto his face. He was asleep without the tubes. Bobby felt a rush of excitement when he realised Jay didn't need the machines any more.

'I brought you a Pepsi.'

He did his magic trick to stop it spilling, and the noise the lid made was amplified by the silence.

'And I brought you the trophy.'

Bobby pulled the sheet back and put the trophy alongside Jay.

'I wore your vest. You're going to love it. It has your initials on it.'

Bobby dipped his little finger into the can and let a drop fall on Jay's lips. He expected to see that cheeky smile. There was no reaction at all. The black drop dripped down Jay's lip and rested on his chin, before falling sideways down his face. Bobby heard the unmistakeable sound of sobbing. The repetitive breaths in, followed by the repetitive breaths out. It got louder and louder. Bernie walked in with a priest dressed in black, and a nurse dressed in white on either side of her. It was like they were holding her up, but she was walking. She looked up and saw Bobby.

'No,' she screamed. 'Please God, no.'

'What's wrong?' asked Bobby.

The priest got down on his hunkers and looked Bobby in the eye.

'Jay passed away.'

'But I brought him a Pepsi. Try giving him the Pepsi,' said Bobby, getting agitated.

He took the can and tried to pour it in Jay's mouth. It fizzed up on his lips and spilled down his face.

'Bobby, he's dead,' shrieked Bernie.

'No, he's not. He needs the Pepsi. Give him the Pepsi.'

Bobby tried to give Jay another drink. The priest grabbed his arm and took the can. He held Bobby in a hug. Bobby didn't want to be hugged by him. Or anybody. Jay couldn't be dead. He was only thirteen.

Bobby wriggled free and ran past Bernie and the nurse. He didn't stop running. He ran outside. He didn't have his bag with him. It didn't matter. He ran as fast as he could, down the canal over the bridge, down Sackville Avenue and home. He stood outside his house and looked around. These streets were his, and Jay's. Jay couldn't be dead.

'Show me the trophy.'

Laura was delighted and she wanted Bobby to be, too.

'I left it with Jay.'

'You went to the hospital?'

She looked at him for a moment, not sure if he was messing or not. Bobby felt his brain changing. It started to tingle.

'How could you get to the hospital and back so quick?' asked his dad.

Why did that matter? thought Bobby. His throat had dried up and he couldn't answer.

'Jay is dead,' he managed to get out.

He sat down on the edge of the couch. His mother jumped down on the floor in front of him.

'Oh, Jesus. Oh Lord Jesus Christ,' she cried out.

His mam never even went to church.

Bobby prayed to Jay, asking him to stop the flow of pee. Jay answered and he was dry. For the first time ever, Bobby heard someone downstairs before him. His mam read out loud the article that mentioned Jay in the paper. She showed him the death notice. It said there would be a wake at Jay's address, followed by funeral mass in St Agatha's Church. Bobby could see huge black bags under his mam's eyes. She worried about most things all the time, so he knew she was horrified by what had happened.

'What's a wake?'

'The wake is where they lay the body out in the home of the family for people to come and pay their respects.'

'And it stays in the house for two days?'

'It does. It's an older way of doing things. When someone so young dies, it's a nice way of allowing people to pay their respects.'

Bobby thought it was ironic that laying a dead body out was called a wake. Why didn't they call it a sleep?

Bobby was nervous before going up to the flat. He was made to wear his Confirmation suit. His mam and dad held hands as they walked him down the avenue. Bobby walked behind them, thinking about how he had held hands with Jay when they jumped off the wall of the paper factory. From the bottom of Sackville Avenue, he could see there was a queue coming out the bottom of the stairwell, and out onto the street. Bobby thought of the number of times he had raced Jay up and down stairwells. He wasn't sure if he wanted to see Jay's dead body again. He heard Jay's voice in his head. 'Don't chicken out now. Come and see me.'

He turned around and saw Anto standing behind him. Anto shook hands with Bobby's mam and dad. Nobody was talking. People were walking down the stairwell with their heads bowed, not making eye contact with anyone. The line moved slowly but, before he knew it, Bobby was at the front door. He could feel himself welling up. He didn't want to cry, but he knew he had no control over his tears. A few people were standing on the stairs   inside the flat. He could see the coffin laid out in the living room. He couldn't see inside it from where he was standing, but he could see it was surrounded by flowers and people. Inside the living room, people paused at the right-hand side of the coffin, and said a prayer, before moving around to pay their condolences to Bernie. Bobby blessed himself the way Jay had shown him. Three taps of the hands together and then he kissed them. Jay was wearing a navy suit Bobby had never seen him in before. He had a white shirt and red tie on. The tie was on properly, not all over the place. Bobby wanted to loosen so it looked like his school tie. He closed his eyes and spoke to Jay in his head.

I hope you can hear me.
You were the most amazing friend anyone could ever
have.
I'm sorry I didn't save you.
I miss you more than anything in the world.
There'll never be anyone else like you.
The flats will miss you and I'll miss you.
Thanks for never calling me a piss-in-the-bed.

He opened his eyes and thought he saw Jay's cheeky smile. He leaned down and kissed him on the forehead. Three teardrops fell on his face. He didn't want to move away as he knew it would be the last time he would ever see him. His feet were frozen to the spot. He felt his dad's hand on his shoulder, pressing him forwards. He took a few steps and found himself in front of Bernie.

'I'm sorry, Bernie.'

She stood up and hugged him, whispering in his ear.

'You have nothing to be sorry for. I have your jersey on his bed. Why don't you go up and get it. He loved when you two were up there together.'

She hugged him again before talking to Matt and Laura. Bobby made his way upstairs. The Liverpool shirt was on the bed. Beside it was his trophy. He opened the drawer on Jay's locker and saw the picture Jay had of the Ballybough United team. Of all the boys in the picture, Jay was the happiest. He had his arm around Bobby in the back row. Everyone else looked very serious. Jay looked like he had been told the funniest joke he had ever heard. That is the way he always was, smiley Jay. Bobby was glad he had got one last smile from him. Underneath the photo was the tape box where he kept his money. He picked it up, and saw that there was something still inside. Then the door opened. He grabbed his jersey and covered the tape box.

'Are you all right Bobby?' asked Anto.

'Yeah.'

'I'm sorry.'

Bobby didn't answer him.

'I'm sorry I couldn't do anything to save him.'

Anto left him alone, the way he wanted it. He opened the tape box and could see the packages that Jay had taken squashed into the notes. Bobby closed it and held it to his chest. He slid it into the inside pocket of his jacket.

He picked up the Liverpool shirt and gripped it as hard as he could. He could see his mam and dad from the top of the stairs. They were talking on the balcony outside the front door. Bobby got to the front door and turned left back towards the coffin. He had the folded shirt in his hands. He skipped to the front of the line, and placed the shirt at Jay's side. He touched his hand off Jay's and walked by

Bernie again. She reached out and grabbed him, nearly bear-hugging him to death.

'He'll be glad you did that. He can wear it in heaven.'

'He'll be captain of the team.'

Bobby took the suit off and hung it back in his wardrobe. He never wanted to wear it again. He took the tape box out and opened it. He counted the money. There was one hundred and fifty pounds. And three lumps of heroin. He put it under the floorboards in the corner of the room where his dad always put the mousetraps. There was an old trap still there with what was once a lump of cheddar cheese on it.

He lay on the bed and thought about whether he would rather be with Jay in heaven or playing in Ballybough without him. He wasn't sure of the answer. He thought about whether it was Anto's fault that Jay was dead. He thought and thought. It was all he could do. He didn't ask to go out because he had nobody to hang around with. He stared out his window at Croke Park, with an endless supply of moments to remember. He laughed to himself when he remembered how sick they felt after drinking all the orange juice. He decided he would never snare a pigeon again, though every time he saw a pigeon he would think of Jay. Every time he heard the word Liverpool he saw Jay flying around the pitch in heaven. He thought of all the times he thought of death and never mentioned it to Jay, embarrassed that Jay might never have thought of death.

Everywhere he went he thought of Jay. If he opened his eyes, he saw something that reminded him of Jay. Every time he closed them, he saw a past memory of Jay. When he lay on his bed looking at the laths above him, he got sad. He touched where he had written Jay's initials. He tried counting the laths over and over to stop himself thinking of Jay, but, in a way, he didn't want to stop thinking about him. It made him sad to remember him, but the thought of not remembering him made him even sadder.

Bobby wasn't surprised how many people were at Jay's funeral. His mam told him it was a big deal that somebody so young would die from drugs. The church was packed, with hundreds left outside. He sat seven rows back on the left-hand side. Bernie sat in the front row on the right. Bobby didn't hear anything the priest said. Bobby counted how many people were in each row, and how many rows there were. He saw the two detectives sitting together, just staring straight ahead. At the end, people went up to shake Bernie's hand. Bobby didn't want to. He had cried enough, and didn't want to get upset again. At the burial in

Glasnevin Cemetery, the sun shone down while it lashed rain at the same time. Bernie screamed at the sight of Jay's coffin joining his father's. It was a scream Bobby had never heard before. It echoed around the gravestones. Bobby just wanted to leave. He had cried himself dry. His eyes stung and his head ached. His dad threw a handful of muck into the hole in the ground after the coffin was lowered. Bobby felt a frozen fear, the thought of looking into the dark hole was too much for him to contemplate.

CHAPTER 14

Bobby stayed in his room, and remembered only the happy thoughts about Jay. He went over full days' adventures in his head. He reckoned he could fill his mind with amazing thoughts of Jay for the rest of his life. He knew he would never forget about him, not one minute would go by for the rest of his life, that he wouldn't think about Jay.

The quiet was broken by four solid knocks on the front door. Bobby heard someone come in, but he didn't go out to the landing to check who it was. He was too drained to care. It was about ten minutes later when he heard his mother coming up the stairs. She always said to him that he sounded like a herd of elephants going down the stairs; she sounded like a herd coming up.

'Can you come downstairs, please?'

'Why?'

'The detectives want to ask you a few more questions.'

He didn't answer, he just followed her down, mimicking her footsteps.

'Hello, Bobby,' McNeill said.

He wondered if Burns did any talking at all. He nodded at McNeill. He didn't even try to wipe the tears away. He had never felt as exhausted in his life. He didn't know if he would be able to run even a hundred yards.

'I don't know if you know, but we've made some arrests. We have been given some information that could land you in a lot of trouble. We have already talked to your mam and dad, and we told them that the last thing we want is for you to get in trouble. All we need is for you to tell us the truth. We arrested Willo Brown, who told us that Jay, and you, were working for Anto. That you were delivering drugs for him.'

'Tell them that's not true son.'

Bobby could feel himself getting weaker by the second, if that was possible.

'Can I get a drink of water, please?'

'We need you to tell us everything you did for Anto. If you don't want to tell us, which I'm sure is not the case, we'll have to arrest you too. You will probably end up in a children's jail.'

Bobby didn't want to end up in a children's jail. Gringo might be there. He was quickly working out in his head what he should say, and what he shouldn't.

'Anto, it's an evil person who makes children do his dirty work.'

Bobby thought if McNeill knew everything,

then why was he asking questions? He knew Anto wouldn't have said anything. He couldn't believe Jay would have told Willo Brown what they were doing. If he did, Willo must have told the police and ratted on Anto. All Bobby knew was that he wanted it to end.

'Anto asked us to help him with his garden. And to deliver a few videos for him.'

'What type of videos?'

'Boxing videos. We watched a few of them in his house, and he had a few friends who were into boxing too.'

'And these videos, what did they look like?'

Bobby thought this was the stupidest question he had ever heard.

'They looked like videos.'

'Were they in boxes?'

'They were in video boxes.'

'Where did you bring the videos?'

Bobby didn't like Micka or Johnny.

'To a fella called Johnny who lived in the Strand flats. And a fella called Micka who lived in the Sean MacDermott Street flats.'

'How many times did you bring videos to Johnny and Micka?'

The truth was he didn't know exactly how many times. He knew he had made about three hundred pounds, which was sixty deliveries.

'About sixty times.'

'Sixty times?'

'Yes.'

'And how did Anto get you to do this?'

'He would hand us the video and say "Bring this to Micka", or "Bring this to Johnny" and we would do it.'

'The information we have is that you knew what was in the videos. And that Jay, and possibly you too, had then sold some of this to somebody else.'

Bobby knew where the information was coming from now. It was scumbag Willo Brown. He knew Jay had sold some to Willo. Why would Willo tell them that, though? Unless he was trying to save his own ass.

'I don't know what you mean.'

'Bobby, if someone stands up in court and says, "Bobby Ryan was delivering heroin to people", it will stain your character for the rest of your life. It will bring shame on your family.'

'I was delivering boxing videos. I watched the videos.'

'Bobby, Anto is in big trouble. The best thing you could do for the memory of Jay would be to tell the truth. We think Jay got the heroin from one of those videos.'

'Why do you think that?'

'When we arrested Willo Brown, he told us that Jay brought the heroin to him.'

'And he told you about Anto, too?'

'He told us about Anto, and you, and Jay. So we know certain things. Other things we are unsure of. When did you know what was in the videos?'

Bobby couldn't remember when he knew. Jay knew before him.

'Jay said that there must be something in them because when we went to Micka's there were junkies outside the flat.'

'And what did he say then?'

If Bobby admitted he saw Jay opening the video, then his mam would hate him for the rest of his life. If she knew he had known he was delivering heroin, then she would be more disgusted than he could ever imagine. She had warned him about the dangers of drugs. He had never even taken a drag of a cigarette and he was about to admit something far worse.

'He said we should open one and see.'

He could hear his mam gasp. He was afraid to look her in the eye. He picked a knot on the pine table and kept staring at it.

'And when did you open it?'

'I didn't. Jay did. And he closed it straight away again. It was the last delivery I did, because I knew it was wrong.'

'And Jay never took any. Are you sure?'

'He did another two deliveries on his own. So I don't know if he took any.'

'It's possible that Anto could be charged with Jay's death. Maybe not murder, but manslaughter.'

Bobby had heard of manslaughter, but he wasn't sure what it meant.

'Bobby, I know Anto was your friend, but he had you delivering death around the streets of Ballybough. He will have to be punished severely for that. If you saw something in that video, it's evidence we can use against him. It will stop this ever happening to another boy like Jay.'

Bobby had nothing left to lie about. The truth was out. He should have told the truth at the start.

'I have something to show you.'

He sprinted up the stairs and pulled the rug back in the corner. He lifted the floorboard and pulled out the tape box. Inside he had stuffed the money. He opened the box and turned it upside-down. He started to shake it to get the money out. It flew out on the fifth shake and straight into the hole. Followed by one of the packages.

'Bobby, what are you doing?' asked his mam, as she startled him with her silence coming up the stairs.

He quickly let the carpet cover the hole.

'I have something to show them.'

He turned to face her and held his hands behind his back.

'What is it?'

He held out the tape box for her to see.

'Tell them to look inside.'

Laura couldn't resist and looked in herself.

'Oh my God, Lord save us.'

McNeill opened the tape cassette box and took out the packages. He held the drugs in the air.

'If that is good quality heroin, it is worth an awful lot of money.'

'How much?' asked Matt.

Bobby wanted to ask, but didn't dare.

'One of them could be worth two thousand pounds.'

Bobby was working out the value of what they had delivered in his head. His mam said he inherited the maths part of his brain from his father.

'And if there were two in each video, and they were sent with sixty videos, that's about a quarter of a million quid. The dirty bastard sending my son around with that. I'll fucking kill him with my own bare hands.'

Bobby looked at his dad knowing he would kill nobody, and that he had his calculations wrong. He was fifty per cent right.

'We will have him arrested immediately. We'll also need to take you to the station to sign a statement. I'm grateful, Mr and Mrs Ryan. You don't understand how helpful he has been.'

'And what's going to happen with Anto?' asked Matt.

'I can't guarantee that he won't get bail; it's unlikely, but you never know. My advice would be to move house.'

'Leave just like that. Are you saying we are not safe in this area now?' asked Laura.

'And how do we go about leaving just like that?'

'We'll be able to help. Your son's testimony is going to put one of the big guys away.'

McNeill turned to Bobby.

'When it goes to court, we'll need you to tell what happened.'

'I know what testimony means.'

His mam glared at him. The police explained exactly what was going to happen in the police station. Bobby told them the full story. His mother cried through all the details. They wrote a statement that Bobby had to sign. It was eight pages long.

Bobby could tell who the important police were. Everybody stood to attention when the biggest of the lot came into the room. He had a belly the size of a rhinoceros and a different colour badge on his uniform. He didn't talk to Bobby directly, everything was addressed to his parents.

'We can definitely keep Anto Burke in jail for two weeks but there would be a slight chance he could get bail. Only a slight chance. I'm suggesting moving you out of the area before that two weeks is up.'

'And where do you suggest we go?' asked Matt.

'That is for you to decide. We will be able to help with the initial cost of relocating the witness. It's all above board. You pick the house and we will take it from there.'

'As simple as that?'

'Yes.'

'How far away does it have to be?' asked Laura.

'It's up to you. Far enough away from the inner city.'

'I'd need a car and I have a bit of a driving issue.'

Bobby heard his dad explaining about the parking fines and not having the money to pay them. That was no problem either. The fines would be wiped out. All those Friday nights, thought Bobby, missing a few minutes of *A Question of Sport* to pay that swine of a parking fines man at the door, when it didn't matter anyway.

Bobby knew what was in store for him when they got him on his own. A hundred questions, all beginning with 'Why?' He didn't care anymore. He wanted to rewind the clock to the beginning of the summer.

CHAPTER 15

Houses in Ballybough didn't sell. They got boarded up. Bobby thought his mam was living in hope that someone might buy theirs. Two thousand pounds had been a lot to pay for the house when they had bought it. He heard his mam say she would take two thousand pounds for it now, ten years later. His dad said to let it go and be positive about starting a new life somewhere else. He had fully bought into the idea. Staying in the inner city wasn't an option. Clontarf wasn't an option because it was too expensive.

Portmarnock was miles away from the city. More than seven and a half miles away. Bobby ran the whole way the first time they went as a family to visit the house. The rest of the family drove in his dad's new car. A brown Fiat 128. Bobby thought he could outrun the car it was such a banger. He bet his dad a pound he could beat the 'shitmobile' with a thirty-minute head start. Portmarnock was on the coast. The run took Bobby along the same route he ran with Anto and Jay many times. Anto would take them over the wooden bridge to Bull Island and along the sandy beach. They would turn around and jog all the way back to Ballybough.

Bobby was running away from Ballybough and it didn't feel right. He stopped at the wooden bridge and held on to the side. He bounced up and down and tried to make it shake. There was no nervous knot in his stomach. There was just a terrible sadness in his heart.

Portmarnock had a beach so long you couldn't see one end from the other. There were loads of fields. And a shop. Which in Bobby's eyes constituted nothingness. A wild nothingness. It was a place where you couldn't walk to somewhere else. You had to take the bus. Bobby and Jay had never even been on the 23 bus that went up and down Ballybough Road. They only ever mooned it. In Ballybough, Bobby could walk over the bridge into Summerhill and it was different. The canal was different. The railway tracks were different. The city centre was different. Every day was different. Every day in Portmarnock would be the same.

The house was in an estate called Carrickhill. When Bobby got there, he sat on the granite block that had the name of the estate engraved on it. It was surrounded by little flowers of all colours. He knew his mam would love it. There wasn't a pigeon in sight. Bobby didn't think the Fiat 128 would fit in with all the other cars. Just like he wouldn't fit in.

Number 62 Carrickhill Walk had three bedrooms and was semi-detached. This was a big deal. So was the fact that the bedrooms were huge, and there was a shower. And that he wouldn't have to share a bedroom any more. He kept those thoughts to himself and found it hard to get excited about their new rented house.

A large truck came to take all the boxes from the house on Ardilaun Road. Eileen and Ned came out to say goodbye. Michael Dunne managed to make it to the front door for the first time in six years. Even though he had the district nurse coming to him, Bobby's dad was his real minder. Bobby had lit Mr Dunne's fire many times on those freezing cold winter evenings, when Matt would make sure to keep it topped up through the night. He could see real emotion in his father's eyes when Mr Dunne stood at the door, using a cane to hold himself up on one side, and the doorframe to hold him up on the other. Bobby couldn't believe he hadn't been at his front door in that long. He wasn't able to step out onto the street. Bobby knew it was his fault that Mr Dunne would miss his dad. And his naggins of whiskey.

Bobby wanted to take the laths off the bed but wasn't allowed. He negotiated to take one.

Everything was in the truck before they knew it. All that was left was to leave Ballybough for the last time. Close the front door and their lives in Ballybough were over.

'One more thing,' shrieked Bobby as he squeezed past his dad and ran up the stairs to his room. He pulled back the rug to reveal the floor-boards one last time. He took out the wad of notes. All that was left was an old mousetrap and a packet of heroin. And a pissy mattress and an empty wardrobe. Bobby took one last look out the window at Croke Park.

'Pull it shut after you,' said his mam as he came out the front door for the last time.

He grabbed the cold brass door handle with both his hands and pulled the door shut. The knocker jumped off the door and tapped the plate twice before resting in place, just like it always did.

CHAPTER 16

Bobby stopped wetting the bed. His new mattress hadn't smelled a drop of his bladder. He changed the words 'Our Father' to 'Our Jay, who art in heaven' in his prayers. He answered every time. He still woke up no later than six in the morning. He would go running before the sun had a chance to rise above the horizon. Just him and a few horses. He would try to step in the hoof prints that they made as their owners galloped them along the   deserted beach. Bobby could see himself changing. He started to get hair on his legs. He didn't like them. Every time some appeared he would shave them off with his brother's razor. He knew Kevin would go mad if he found out, but the bathroom door had a lock, and he made sure to clean all the hairs out of the blade, and to put it back in exactly the same position he found it in. Jay had said he hated hairy legs.

Normally September was the month Bobby hated the most. Going back to school after a summer playing with Jay. Now August was his most hated month because of what had happened. Bobby refused to go to his new school. It was a protest he knew he couldn't keep up forever, but one that he knew his parents would have sympathy for. He knew they were concerned for him. He never used to stay in his room in Ballybough, now it was all he did.

'You'll fall behind. You will end up being kept back a year if you don't go to school,' his mam would tell him.

Bobby didn't care. Having to memorise all the names of the mountains and rivers in Ireland was stupid. The best river in Ireland was the Tolka and it wasn't even on any of the maps. Neither was the canal. His mam agreed that he could stay at home for a few weeks, but he had to study in his room. Bobby couldn't study. All he could do was think of Jay. He would close his eyes and relive everything they did together. He could remember everything about Ballybough. The colours of the front doors, the cracks on the footpaths and the sound of Jay's voice.

Bobby's protests lasted until the end of October. At that stage Kevin had made new friends who liked Jimi Hendrix and The Doors and played guitars and drums. The noise coming from Kevin's bedroom was deafening. He now had an amp and an electric guitar. Bobby felt like throwing them out the window.

He was not allowed to tell anyone about what had happened in Ballybough. His mam registered him in school as Bobby Shannon, using her surname. He hated it being called out in class. He felt stupid. He wasn't Bobby Shannon, he was Bobby Ryan. Maths was his favourite class. The teacher, Mr Maxwell, would have a quiz every Friday where he called out questions. The fastest to get the correct answer would win a point for their team. Bobby was only allowed to answer every second question because he could get every one correct before his classmates. Everyone would laugh at him for working the questions out so quickly in his head, while they were still writing it down in their copies. They weren't slagging him though.

Gym class was crap. They played hockey and rugby, no football. Or running. He could have played basketball, but all the girls played that. He made up excuses about torn hamstrings and calf muscles. The teacher didn't care if he took part or not. He was allowed to sit alone watching everyone else play. He knew Jay would have liked basketball. If he could jump off high walls, he could probably jump up high to put the ball in the net. He would have loved the girls too. Bobby found it hard to talk to them on his own; if Jay was with him, they would have been the centre of attention.

Bobby eventually did all his schoolwork without complaint. He didn't find it difficult and it took his mind off Ballybough for a while. In school, he found himself talking to the girls more than the boys when he eventually began to find his voice. He couldn't be himself though; none of them were interested in snaring pigeons or jumping off walls or fishing in the canal. There was a group of three boys in his class who thought they were the kings. They started calling him 'Shanno', even though nobody else did. They didn't know he was an All-Ireland boxing champion, until Bobby mentioned it in class one day when asked about his interests. They never called him Shanno again. Bobby realised very quickly it was easy to stay under the radar. Do your homework and don't get in trouble.

Even though he had missed two months of classes, Bobby still got excellent results in his exams. The cold dark mornings of November and December meant he wasn't allowed to run before school. The minute he got home, he would rip off his uncomfortable wine-coloured school jumper, followed by the tie and shirt and horrible grey slacks. He felt comfortable in his runners, shorts and long-sleeved top, even though it was freezing. The minute his bald, white legs hit the winter air, goosebumps would appear everywhere. He had to go fast at the start to warm up, the opposite of what Anto had always told him. He focused on the noise of his feet caressing the pavement or sand. Anto told him to 'run on your toes, feather the ground'. He listened to his nostrils taking in a breath and concentrated on blowing it slowly out his mouth. 'Try and glide along,' Anto would say. Jay never shut up long enough for Bobby to concentrate on anything Anto said to them. He could concentrate enough now. A sixty-minute run would go by before he knew it. Then it was back to the real world.

CHAPTER 17

The canal was full of rats, and now Bobby was going to be one. Jay used to tell Bobby that a rat was the worst thing you could be. If you ratted on someone in the inner city, your name would go up in graffiti with the words 'Rats Out' beside it. This was different though. What Anto did was unforgiveable. It was his name that was put up in graffiti on the pramsheds in Ballybough and on one of the derelict buildings in Summerhill. There were pictures of it in the paper. It was sprayed in blue paint. The article was about the trial and what Anto was accused of. It said he had been one of the major drug dealers in Dublin. Bobby couldn't help thinking that if Jay had never opened the video, they would both be still be the kings of Ballybough.

Bobby laid his new suit out on the bed for the first time. It was navy with three buttons on the jacket. He picked it out himself, as well as the white shirt and red tie. His mother loved him in it. She looked at him with a loving smile. He polished his shoes, a pair of black patent leather slip-ons with a tassle on them. His mother thought they were disgusting, which made Bobby want them even more. She wanted him to buy a pair with laces. The slip-ons were shiny enough to see your reflection.

Bobby had been made to sign statements about exactly what had happened. He asked what would happen if he said nothing. The police said he would end up going to a reform school until he was at least eighteen. He knew that would end his chances of running in the Olympics. They said they needed him to testify or Anto would get off. He was given the list of questions he would be asked, and he had to practise the answers to a man wearing a stupid wig and a black cape. The first question was going to be easy, building up to the deliveries, the stolen heroin, and finding Jay in the unknown house. He would have to point at Anto and say 'it was him who gave us the videos'.

An unmarked police car collected them at 8.45 a.m. They were taken to the station, where they were offered breakfast. Bobby couldn't contemplate eating anything; he asked for a glass of water, which he sipped, while his parents drank cups of tea. The tea wasn't made the way his dad liked it. The youngest of the policemen stirred the cup and just took the bag out without squeezing it. He left a trail of drops on the table. His dad would get every drop out of the tea bag. He said each drop was a valuable commodity. His dad was able to eat two slices of white bread, toasted. Bobby could see it was cold, as the butter didn't melt when he put it on with the plastic knife. His mother spent the whole time holding Bobby's hand and making sure he was OK. Every day of the trial so far the papers had run a different story about Anto. Headlines such as 'Children Used to Run Heroin' appeared with Anto's picture. Bobby didn't know what to think. His name didn't appear in the paper because he was under eighteen, but he knew it wouldn't take a Ballybough genius to work out that Jay and himself were the 'teenage boys'.

Bobby was due to take the stand after lunch. Before him, McNeill gave evidence. He told of raiding Anto's house and finding nearly two hundred grams of heroin. He told of the two boys who would deliver the heroin hidden in videos to different dealers around the inner city. He said that one of the runners would testify in court that he saw heroin in the video box after his best friend opened it.

Matt decided they would go to the Bad Ass Café in Temple Bar for some food. Bobby's dad had once won money on the football pools one Saturday and had taken them there. Bobby loved their pizzas. The waiter would write the order on a docket similar to the one used in Ladbrokes. He would then reach up in the air, where there was a pulley system. The docket went into a holder, which was screwed into a socket. The socket had a string hanging down from it. Bobby and Kevin would always fight over who would get to pull the string. The waiter would lift one of them up to pull it. It flew across the restaurant above their heads to the order counter.

Detective McNeill accompanied them. He ordered a pizza to start and lasagne for a main course. Bobby looked at his stomach and thought he might need two pizzas and two lasagnes to fill the mound that came out over his belt. Bobby ordered an American cheeseburger. It was twice the price of the pizza. He knew he wouldn't be able to eat anything, but because McNeill was paying he ordered the most expensive thing on the menu. And a Coke. He could drink that. His stomach just wasn't capable of taking food in.

Bobby was in his own world, caught up in his own thoughts. He couldn't stop thinking about Jay and how he had ended up going to the unknown house. And his mam's comments about how he was different to the boys in the flats. On the way back to the court, they all walked under the arch and over the Ha'penny Bridge. Bobby said a little prayer to Jay and asked him for help. He didn't know what to do. It wasn't supposed to be like this.

They walked down the river away from the city centre towards the large, grey, concrete court building. Michael Dunne had told him a story about when he was a boy during the Civil War in the 1920s. He remembered the bombing of the Four Courts. Bobby wished that the building would be bombed before they got back. They walked inside and onto the cold marble floor. There were people milling about everywhere. A man in a wig approached them and said there was an adjournment for legal argument.

The pillars in the court were about the same thickness as the conker trees in Holy Cross College. Bobby thought about Jay climbing the trees. He had reminded him of a monkey in the zoo. He had never looked down and had never shown any fear. He had just laughed and had shouted at Bobby, 'Come on you chicken!' Jay had given Bobby the courage he hadn't had before. He had always tried to beat his fear and climb higher because he hadn't wanted to bottle it in front of Jay. Bobby knew that the higher he went, the farther the fall. Jay had always said, 'The higher you get, the better the view.'

Bobby hadn't been back to Ballybough and he missed it. He didn't think you could miss a place like a person, but he did. There was something special about Ballybough, just like there was something special about Jay. He missed the sprints to the shop and the laps around Croker. And he never stopped missing Jay. He missed Jay more than anything else. He would trade all the money in the world to have Jay back. He talked to him all day, every day.

'I'm coming to see you.'

Bobby ran out the main door and past more conker-tree pillars. He started jogging down the River Liffey towards the city centre. He didn't want to stop. He jogged all the way to O'Connell Bridge. He turned into O'Connell Street. It was less than a mile long. He could feel the sweat building up on his back, so he took the jacket off and tied it around his waist.

He ran all the way to Dorset Street. His feet began to ache because his new shoes had only been worn twice. He could feel the blisters beginning to take shape on his heels. He would normally feel out of breath after a few miles as his heart rate increased. He didn't now: he felt like he could keep on running forever. Anto had shown him he could run much faster than he had ever thought possible. He crossed the bridge and jogged up the canal bank towards their favourite fishing spot. There were two boys a bit younger than him fishing in the canal. He slipped off his shoe and saw a dark wet patch on his sock. He took his sock off and looked at the blister. It was perfectly round. He wondered why blisters were always that shape. He had the menu from the Bad Ass in his pocket. It was the size of an A4 sheet. He tore it in half and folded each sheet in half again and again to make them small enough to fit into his shoes. He slid them down into the back of his heel to limit the rubbing of the blisters.

Bobby sat on the edge of the canal bank and stared into the water. It was too dark to see any fish, unless they swam right up to the surface. He let the soles dangle just above the water. Bobby could see his reflection on his shoes and in the water. He let a spit dangle from his lips. It hung on for dear life before dropping into the water, causing a small ripple. Then a perch swam up to the surface. It hovered, just breaking the surface of the water with its top lip. Bobby thought he could see the perch smile at him before it turned and swam back into the darkness. He took a few steps back and found himself jogging towards the cemetery. Glasnevin Cemetery was about a mile from the canal.

Bobby slowed to a walk when he got to the main gates. Just inside was where all the famous people in Irish history were buried. There were yellow letters on the wall of the cemetery. Find AK, then take a right and Jay's grave was about fifty metres down on a corner. He knew there would be flowers on the grave. Bobby saw two magpies sitting on the branch of a large tree, chattering loudly. Two for joy, thought Bobby. The magpies were taking turns chattering. It sounded like they were imitating each other, like Jay imitated the culchies when they came to Croke Park. Under the tree, Bobby saw fresh flowers beside a shiny black headstone.

He read the gravestone. It said 'Donie McCann, loving father, brother and son. Tragically killed 13th February 1977.' Underneath it said 'Jason McCann, a sad loss of a young life, 14th August 1985.'

There was a photo of Jay inset on the gravestone. It was from the Ballybough United photo of smiley Jay. Bobby could see part of his own arm around Jay's shoulder. His infectious smile showing his big white teeth. Bobby knelt down on the side of the grave and closed his eyes.

I miss you Jay, I miss you. Why are you gone? We could have been playing football together, or winning tree-climbing competitions. Well, you could have been winning them. I would have been second. There'll be no more rafts on the Tolka, or racing down the stairwells in the flats. No more snaring pigeons. No more derelict houses. No more robbing jeans, for you. No more chicken shit for me.

The two magpies flew away. He felt a presence beside him. He looked around and there was nobody there. He took his jacket off, folded it in half and placed it on the grave.

You can't run in those shoes, Bobby!

How could he still hear Jay's voice so clearly? He wondered if it would ever go away. He never wanted it to. Bobby blessed himself with his right hand. Jay always said it was bad luck to bless yourself with your left. He touched his hands three times together and kissed them. Jay did it before every match; he even did it when he was fishing to bring himself luck. Bobby said a little prayer for God to look after Jay in heaven. And to make sure he was on the football team, because he was fit and would run rings around everyone. It was his favourite thing to do. If he was through on goal and you were chasing him down, he would turn and knock the ball through your legs and laugh, rather than kick it into the net.

The state of your tie.

Bobby loosened the tie and pulled the loop over his head. He hung it from the corner of the headstone. He started jogging. His feet began to move like they were feathering the ground, Dubarry shoes or not. He felt like he was floating, floating all the way back to Ballybough.

He ran down Sackville Avenue, past Jay's flat and the unknown house and stood outside his old home. Sweat was pouring from his face and his shirt was stuck to his back. The front of the house was boarded up, so he climbed into the back garden. Smartie was still jumping up the wall. Bobby pulled the bathroom window open and squeezed himself backwards into the small gap. His shoes dropped into the bath, sliding as they came into contact with the thick dust that had formed. He turned the cold tap and water spluttered out. He clasped his fingers together and splashed his face with as much of the water as his small hands could hold. He picked up the dirty glass that had held the family's toothbrushes and filled it with water.

Upstairs, a small beam of light came through the open bedroom door and shone diagonally across the stairs. Bobby could see dust floating through the beam. He reached out to grab some, but the motion of his hand just blew it all away. The smell of the piss-in-the-bed mattress hadn't gone away. The large stain in the middle of it had formed a crust. It was dark green. How could an orange mattress turn dark green, thought Bobby. He pushed open the window and let some air in. He lay on the very edge of it and looked up at the fifteen laths. The missing one was under his bed in Portmarnock.

Jay had said that he had seen his dad in heaven when he was in the unknown house. Maybe Bobby could visit Jay in heaven. Just once, he thought. He pulled back the rug to see the mousetrap for the last time. He took out the packet of heroin and put it in his mouth. He was feeling tired from all his running. He closed his eyes and let the lump fall onto his tongue. He played with it in his mouth like it was a golfball chewing gum. He took a slug of water and swallowed. Gone. He lay on the bed and closed his eyes.

The memories of Jay fought with the pain in his stomach. The memories were winning and started flooding back one after another. Hundreds of them. His mind didn't pause on one memory for too long. Bobby felt his body floating through the red BRs and JMcCs on the laths above. Then he saw more red and the number seven. It was his Liverpool shirt. Jay turned and passed the ball to him. He passed it back to Jay, who chipped it back again. Bobby took it down on his chest and passed it back to Jay, who volleyed it into the top corner of the net. Bobby ran towards Jay, who was kissing the crest on his Liverpool shirt. Bobby went to jump on his back, but his body floated through Jay's. He turned and looked Jay in the eyes. The smiley eyes. The big white teeth. He reached out to grab the smiley face.

'Good to see you again, Bobby.'
'I missed you.'
'I missed you, too.'